MISTER MANN

Gerrard G. Gerrard attempted suicide at the age of ten. His first novel, *Mister Mann*, is a humorous heartfelt apology to all those who may have been affected by his selfishness. He has written four sitcoms, one film script, a children's book and two other novels: *Mann Online* and *The Fool*. He has been an *Avon* lady, a soldier, a scientist, an apprentice astronaut, a magician, an adventurer and a fund manager. He lives in the country with a cocker spaniel named Carlos.

REVIEWS

'*Mister Mann* takes us on a journey into the darkest recesses of our own psyche. The darkness of *Se7en* and the humour of *The Big Lebowski*. Truly a modern great.'

- *Raymond Brown*

'*A Clockwork Orange* molests *Bambi*!'

- *Linda Bianchi*

'Think *The Wasp Factory* meets *Fight Club* meets *Stone Junction* meets magician Paul Daniels if he were on acid.'

- *Arran Lamont*

'...a truthful philosophical work.'

Dylan Grice

'*Mister Mann* is a witty, richly dark and brutal piece... '

- *Suzi Jones*

'...an hallucinatory trawl through the worst of inhuman fantasy and the best of human understanding.'

H.L. Brooks

MISTER MANN

Gerrard G. Gerrard (signature)

Gerrard G. Gerrard

PRONOIA

Published by Pronoia Books © 2012

First published in the UK in 2009 by Pronoia Books

PO Box 106, Manchester, M32 8RG, UK

www.pronoia-records.com

ISBN 978-0-9569290-2-0

Original cover photograph by Rich Simic
Interior images by permission *Dreamstime* ©

Dedicated to the memory
of Andy Wilkins,
the biggest cunt I know.

PART

ONE

D R E A M

What is it, by knowing which, you will know everything?

I had that dream again last night. It was the usual start, me and Monica getting it on. I say I'm going to spurt soon but not to worry as I'll be ready to go again after five minutes and I intend to fill her up with my white hot love lava. She purrs. I then tell her that I'll start on her Aristotle and after turning it into a brimming cauldron of man porridge I'll give her a face like a decorator's wireless. She squeals with delight.

'After all, I am the Queen of Arse,' she says, weakly trying to pun on the Princess Diana 'Queen of Hearts' motif. Monica was a lot of things, God bless her, but a comedienne she wasn't.

The door bursts open and standing there are World leaders, religious figures and men of import. They are not happy and want me dead. I ask Monica if she minds if I go into battle and, smiling through sticky eyes, she gives me full encouragement. So, naked I charge the first in line.

Terrorists: Osama, Hamza, Arafat and Mandela, my engorged manhood wanting action, but not in a homosexual way. And I give it to them. Hamza, realising his hook is having no effect, starts swapping it for sex toys. He goes through the full *Ann Summers* range before recognising that this is just giving me more power. My only weapons are my hands, feet and two heads. So I set about giving them all love. Pretty soon the terrorists are covered in Mister Mann muck, sitting back smoking *Gitanes* - all relaxed smiles and nodding approval at my prowess. Osama winks at me, his nose runs, there's admiration in his eye but also a hint of fear and concern for me. He knows the next wave is going to be tougher. Lovely kissable lips Osama, enough to turn any man's head.

In walk the clerics of the West: Rumsey, assorted leaders of the one hundred or so top world religions, and the Pope (not sure which one, they all look the same to me, lovely dress though; flowing, light, figure hugging). Same memo: two hands, two feet, two heads and lots and lots of love. I cover them all even quicker this time, my power increasing. I'm in constant vinegar strokes and no sign of *le petite mort*. Everywhere satisfied dripping and smiling holy men smoking *Gitanes*.

Then the world leaders arrive: Bush, Brown, Putin and thousands of others. Same result. All saturated in Mister Mann protein, smoking and smiling. It took even less time than the previous wave.

And then it was time for my usual shower, the vest I was wearing was covered in terrorist beard hair, politicians' dribble and spleen blood from the clergy. Usual process, I take a vest off and another appears in its place, I grow annoyed as I want to get clean. I take the other vest off, and another appears. The more vests I take off the harder they become to remove. I end up tearing them off, in a mad angry frenzy, the hair, spit, and blood increasing with every vest. I am filthy, dripping in stench.

And then something different happens. I decide to enter the shower fully clothed. The vest disappears, my clothes disappear and I am refreshed by the water cascading on my flesh and instead of waking up with a feeling of lack and wanting, I have a sense of overwhelming peace and joy.

I think I'm turning a corner.

2

R O G E R S

And now you are judging me. You are discriminating, which is good. Keep that going, but be prepared to change your view.

I blame my parents. They fuck you up, as Ted Hughes said. Or was it Ted Rogers? Probably originally Rogers and Hughes nicked it - Hughes lounging in the green room, smoking his *Gauloises* and looking camply Northern, waiting for his mate Ted to finish up on the set of *3-2-1*. In walks Rogers.

'Oi Ted, aye oop!'

'Aye oop Ted! Did they get the clue about the penguin bashing the seal with the Eskimo?'

'Nah mate, nice riddle you wrote there, well done.'

'Nae worries, me old whippet, but it's not exactly what I want to do, write naff riddles for a game show.'

'Oh yeah mate, and what exactly *do* you want to do?'

'I want to be the Poet Laureate.'

'Get to fuck!'

'I do! Wanted it all me life. That'd show me dad for calling us the ponce with the pen.'

'Look at us, Ted. You're a camp northern poet and I'm a fooking spastic game show host. I wanted to be a greengrocer. Something simple and satisfying. But look at us! Talk about wanting approval. Aye Ted, they fuck you up, your mum and dad.'

'That's good mate, can I nick it?'

'Knock yourself out me old aye-oop-black-pudding, I owe you one for the 'All you win is a brand new dustbin!'

catchphrase. It is a fabulous rhyme, mate!'

But I digress. It wasn't Hughes, it was Larkin, and Larkin hated Rogers. And he smoked *Rothmans*.

As a child I was abused. Not sexually abused, it was much worse. I was physically abused. At least with sexual abuse you might get a few kind words of encouragement and eventually a chance to cum. With physical abuse all you get is a chance to bleed. Retreat to that place where He can't hurt you, and bleed.

The people I have discussed this with, the sexually abused, always disagree. They say the mental scarring, guilt and shame are far worse. But you get all that with the physical abuse, and big bruises and broken bones too. I used to argue for hours with my sister about it. We never saw each other's point of view. I used to complain that at least she got a cuddle and the occasional guilt-inspired present, but she'd fly off the handle and hit me. Hit me. She knew I was being physically abused and she hit me. I'd a good mind to cum in her face to get my own back. Women, eh! I suppose we all think our problems are a lot worse than they really are.

The good thing about the abuse is that it has taught me to read people, get in tune with their moods very quickly, empathise with them. It is important to read moods when you are seconds away from a beating. Sometimes you can persuade someone not to strike, at the very least you can position your body for minimal damage; it's the difference between a cracked rib and a crushed cranium.

I bet Ted Rogers knew all about reading people. I met him once when I was working on the Portsmouth to Isle of Wight hovercraft. I was a baggage boy, fourteen years old, he was getting on the hovercraft and we all shouted 'Where's

Dusty Bin?' How we laughed. I'll never forget his quizzical look as he turned to give the familiar lightning-fast *3-2-1* hand gesture. The other baggage boys had drawn a large elaborate penis on my face as part of a bizarre initiation ceremony; the shaft emerging from my mouth, the ball sack resting on my chin. The pubescent bum fluff I had so far developed gave it an eerie life-like quality. I had also only just emerged from the sea, having been thrown off Clarence Pier as part of the rite, and the way the water droplets rolled and formed on my face gave a 3D effect to the inked cock - very realistic. Poor Ted looked shocked at the sight of a drenched pubescent boy with a dismembered member in his mouth. That was the only time in his career that he cocked up the *3-2-1* hand gesture, apparently.

Ted left Portsmouth and the lads set on me and gave me a good thrashing. They were a bit upset that I'd taken three of them with me off Clarence Pier and into the sea and wanted to teach me a lesson. Ten of them gave me a fine kicking, but it was nothing compared to Him. So I laughed it off and called them all ponces. That earned me respect, but I never became popular. The bigger lads would occasionally try to make me cry by punching me unexpectedly during the quiet times. They never managed it. I loved that place, I felt accepted at last. They were happy days.

GERRARD G. GERRARD

3

A P P R O V A L

So, wanting approval, why do we bother? I desperately wanted to be popular with the lads down the terminal, but I was no good. I couldn't play sport, I wasn't smart and interesting, I couldn't play a musical instrument, I had no natural charisma; I was odd. The only skills I had were reading people and defence. I couldn't even fight properly; I had no attack instinct left. I decided to do what all kids who have absolutely no social skills do, I became a magician. But unlike most magicians I used the magic to learn social skills. I was good from the start and became expert quickly. The ability to read people helped. I particularly liked the mind-reading stunts. But they only made me appear weirder so I settled for the Tommy Cooper stuff to ingratiate myself with my audience. I was useful. I would clown and make girls laugh so the others could get in their knickers. I learnt all kinds of psychological nuisances from conjuring, most too numerous and dull to mention. But one that stuck was this: that people thought, truly believed, their minds were perfect. The mind is not perfect; it is full of redundant programs and so very fragile. The mind is very easily fooled. People are stupid, really thick. Pointing that out got me into trouble. I'd make something disappear and reappear (by means of distraction and manipulation) and people could not work it out. Some would actually believe the thing had vanished. And more astonishing, weeks later I would be asked to repeat a trick that had been so distorted in the spectator's mind, that not even Copperfield with all his gadgetry and big budgets could reproduce it.

'No. I didn't do that.'

'Yes you did! It was brilliant! Ah, I get it, magicians' code, can't repeat the same trick twice and all that.'

'No, you cunt. What you described is impossible. This is what I did, you stupid, thick, moronic twat.'

'Not bad, but not as good as the trick you did last week.'

'Fer fuck's sake, out of all the spunk your mum had up her she had to make you!'

Women say that men improve with age. The reason for this is that we figure out that women are stupid and not worth pursuing, then we leave them alone. It's nothing personal. That's why women like homosexuals. Gays have no interest in tits and vag, they like chocolate and shoes. Women are rarely harassed sexually by inane chatter about *Godiva* and *Gucci*.

It's why old men need *Viagra*. You can be the most beautiful woman in the world, but if you are ugly inside it shows to the wise. My sister says this is utter rubbish. Is she saying our granddad wouldn't bang the shit out of Claudia Schiffer if only looks counted? Of course he would, but he knows through experience that all people are worthless and so occupies himself in his allotment shed having a crafty wank over the latest developments in particle physics. Stick that in your Popperian cosmology pipe, Karl, and smoke it like your first falsifiable cock; hesitant at first, rising to a peak of joyous understanding and slobbering enthusiasm.

Why is *New Scientist* the most popular magazine in the world? OAPs jodding off to robotic and nanotech specials, that's why. Granddad doesn't tell anyone because he can't be bothered and most won't believe him so he blames it on his plumbing. Then *Viagra* comes along and grandma gets on granddad's case, and instead of telling her to poke it he feels guilty and bows to the pressure, proving once again that people are shit. There's an upside to *Viagra*; granddad can now get through a whole *New Scientist* and half a *National Geographic* before his yoghurt rocket runs out of fuel. Very useful for whiling away those long, deadly boring retirement years.

GERRARD G. GERRARD

4

C O N T R O L

And now you are judging me. You are discriminating, which is good. Keep that going, but be prepared to change your view.

My interest in magic earned me approval. I was ready for control. I wanted control. I became fascinated that everyone liked my tricks and clowning except Him. As I was growing in size and confidence the beatings became less, but when they did come they were more severe, repressed, vicious. I started to wonder about my inability to attack. I could predict when someone would strike and I'd move, not be there, diffuse; no one could touch me except Him. It was a puzzle, why did I let Him? I wanted to learn to fight.

I joined several martial arts classes and studied hard. The characters of the arts can be determined simply by walking into the changing rooms.

Karate - neat, ordered individuals, two in the corner taking it in turns to punch each other in the stomach. Blocky, rigid people, always someone doing three hundred sit ups. Ridiculous.

Kung Fu - mostly Asians, their lovely silky hair combed to perfection, several preening in the mirror, flicking hair, flicking feet and fists. It was all very vain. Deadly, but essentially foppish.

Judo - good eggs, down to earth. They liked the art for the mechanics, not to prove something. Likewise with Ju-Jitsu, but that lot were a bit more likely to eat kebabs.

And then I finally found Aikido. There was only one

person in the changing room; a pot-bellied sixty year-old smoking an *Embassy Number 6* and drinking real ale. That was my instructor. I'll never forget my first lesson. I waited fifty minutes for him to make a move, but he did nothing but talk. My strength was 'defence not attack', although by this time I could attack pretty well. He just smiled and talked the philosophy of fighting, or as he put it, The Art of Peace.

'The Art of Peace begins with you. Work on yourself and your appointed task in the Art of Peace. Everyone has a spirit that can be refined, a body that can be trained in some manner, a suitable path to follow. You are here for no other purpose than to realise your inner divinity and manifest your innate enlightenment. Foster peace in your own life and then apply the art to all that you encounter.'

He just stood there talking and emanating peace. I did not want to attack. I finally asked him to demonstrate something. He approached, talking all the while about taking balance. He placed his hand lightly on my head and I fell. Enraged that he had fooled me, I attacked. He disappeared and I found myself flying ten feet through the air. He appeared at my side and pinned me to the ground with one finger. I could not move.

'Fancy a pint, son? All this fighting has left me gasping.'

We took up the rest of the session in the pub. He thanked me for the challenge, told me he could tell I was useful, that I could handle myself and was a bit tasty. It was a pleasure to be able to mix it with me. Challenge? The old cunt had done me good and proper and I had no idea how. He asked me to think around it. It felt like magic. It was the finest display of magic I had ever seen. But I knew that all magic had a solution. I worked backwards. The pin - that had to be simple mechanics, but one finger, *how*? The flight -

I barely recalled him appearing under me and flicking me on his hips, mechanics again? The initial balance take, mechanics too? But the speed, preternatural, that had to be intuition. He was impressed by my patchy explanation. All his previous students had claimed it was magic, and given him almost god-like reverence, but he couldn't be arsed with all that superstition nonsense so told them to fuck off.

'Whaddya say, son, you want to learn the clever stuff?'

'Fuck yeah, Sensei!'

'If you use that word again, wanker, I'll break your fuckin' neck! The name is Stan.'

'Sorry. Fuck yeah, Stan!'

That's what I liked about Stan, no respect for the traditions. His view of all that Japanese 'be-a-slave-to-the-master-for-years-before-you-are-worthy-to-clean-his-bellend' was that it just created a mass of egos and would do nothing to move the art forward.

'Where's the progress with that 'eventually-after-ten-years-of-sack-scrubbing-you-will-be-drip-fed-the-secrets' bullshit?'

Stan was right. All you'd end up with is a bunch of brainwashed pyjama-wearers who are reasonably adept at doing someone else's Aikido. The true strength is doing your own Aikido. You are the best in the world at being you.

Stan and I practised in all the clubs and bars around Portsmouth. Soon the local hard men knew to leave us alone but there was always a constant stream of foreign sailors eager for a fight. We never started the fights but we never exactly backed down either. Stan loved it. Tearing muscles from arms in a well-timed *kotegaeshi*, slamming heads through plate glass with an *irimi nage*, dislocating shoulders with a rolling lock even when the poor mug had surrendered. He was teaching lessons.

'Never underestimate the fat old cunt of a bloke who has just 'accidentally' spilled your pint.'

If Stan had a fault, it was this: he would often confuse peace with mayhem. But as he would say, 'The countryside is often viewed as a peaceful place to be, somewhere to relax, unwind. But look below the surface and you see all kinds of activity. Bees collecting flower spunk, flowers offering up nectar to the prostitute bee. Millions of insects fornicating madly before their woefully short life spans are up. Birds that provide the sweet songs are really trying to get a shag, or warn competitors off their territory. One man's peace is another man's brothel or war zone, mate.'

I only ever got really excited when glass or a knife was involved, that really focuses the mind and sharpens the predictive sense. I could often get my opponent to cut himself, just by moving a certain way. It's difficult to describe, but by moving around him and gently brushing certain parts of his body, I could infuriate and guide him to use his weapon to harm himself. It was akin to becoming my own opponent and commanding self harm.

Stan taught me well. I was discovering my techniques. But I grew tired of the brutality. I was now moving without effort and with barely any physical involvement. I needed to progress, to somehow remove myself from the fight. Not to hang up my sword and become a monk, like in the clichéd movies, but to move beyond the physical violence and into something special.

Stan had found his level, he relished the coarse brawling. Stan is eighty-five now and still at it.

'I can't give it up, mate; it's just so fuckin' lovely. Moulding with your opponent, becoming one, a real feeling of connection to the Universe. It's like love times a hundred.

Like three hundred *Viagra* tabs and the entire back catalogue of *Scientific America* in one hit. To give it up would be like taking my soul.'

I understood.

GERRARD G. GERRARD

5

S E C U R I T Y

AND now you are judging me. You are discriminating, which is good. Keep that going, but be prepared to change.

Security is the tricky one. How do you become truly secure? I couldn't become secure with Him still there. He had to go.

My only regret was telling my sister. She wasn't ready for the truth and it tipped her further into madness. I knew it would. I knew I would tell her. Ah well, she's in a better place now.

Did I kill Him? Yes and no.

Time is a great healer. It is also an illusion. A very convenient one; without time everything would happen all at once and things could get a bit messy.

Time can be broken down neatly into past, present and future. The only thing that matters is the present because the other two do not exist. The future has not happened yet and is at best mere speculation of the mind. The past is gone, it is only a memory. So what is real? The present? You can make up anything and call it the truth in the present, but the present is not real because it is instantaneously confined to the past.

So, *did* I kill Him? Yes and no.

He had become very much a part of me, a cancer. I understood this cancer and cared for it. He was sick and needed another chance. I was just setting Him free; it was like rebooting a computer really. So no, not killing Him.

Pissing on His mangled twisted body and relishing

the sight of the blood oozing from His twitching corpse. Well yes, killing Him, I suppose. You decide, if you must.

I had discovered my true martial techniques. And He provided the final keys. I'd resolved to get rid of my anger and embrace Him in true love. To love is to understand and I started to understand why He did the terrible things He did. He acted in response to fear, grief, anger, and lust. I finally felt compassion for Him and wanted to help Him along his path to understanding. And so I got close, befriended Him, forgave Him and amplified His already enormous scripts of self-loathing and urged Him to make the right choice.

After three months of preparation He was ready for the final talk. The mind is so fragile.

I had practised on others. I had to make sure my technique was perfect for Him. The others all wanted release. The others were grateful, and I was grateful to them for giving me the chance to hone my art.

'I am so glad we've managed to put all that stuff behind us. I was doing it for your own good. And look, it has worked. You really were an annoying shit, but now look at you! You are the best mate anyone could hope for.'

I smiled. His time had come.

I used what I now call the 'Worthless Script'. I have so many, this was the first.

'You are the only person who understands me.'

That was an understatement. I knew exactly what He was. He was a coward; frightened, alone and craving control. He got his control from violence and repression. He was a wretched waste of life. I also now knew how His mind worked. I knew how to unlock it, how to step in and alter it. I knew how to break it.

'I am so lucky to have you as a friend.'

Yes you are. I can set you free. 'Have you heard of

Elzeard Bouffier?' I said quietly.

'No. Sounds like a pigeon eater. He's not that frog who works on the Portsmouth Le Havre ferry? The one who got done for cocking off in the cream of chicken soup?'

'No. He was a very important man, one of my heroes.'

He had never seen me like this. Usually I was quiet and reserved. More recently I had become calm, soothing, perceptive and healing. Now I was earnest. This was important. He instinctively knew to pay attention. Something deep within him shifted and broke.

'He was a shepherd. One day he realised that the land on which his flock grazed was no longer the land of his youth. It had been rich, abundant with trees, animals and people. It was now barren and colourless, populated by abandoned crumbling stone buildings. Harsh dry winds attacked. This desolate area had been over-worked, the grass, previously verdant, was now scant and worst of all, the beautiful forests that once grew had been cut so that now only a few twisted oaks remained to provide shade.'

I touched His temple. He tranced.

'Bouffier took action. Armed with a bag of acorns and a long cane he began to plant trees. As he roamed the hills with his sheep, he would occasionally make a hole in the ground with the cane and drop an acorn. He asked no one's permission. He just did it. He planted thousands of acorns.'

His catalogue of violence flashed within Him; the constant beatings given to His younger brother, the hatred shown to all His lovers, the rape of His little sister. Blaming, and shifting responsibility. Shuffle and reshuffle. It was not His fault.

I stroked His brow with the back of my hand. The

broken thing splintered.

'He did this for forty years. Gradually the trees grew; oak saplings took root in the valley, providing shade and moisture. Bouffier gave up being a shepherd because he was worried about the sheep affecting his young trees. He became a beekeeper, aiding pollination and growth. New streams began to run through the valley. Peace and beauty of the regenerating land encouraged animals to return.'

I passed my hands in front of His eyes and gently closed His lids.

'By 1945 another war was over. This old shepherd was still planting - oak, beech, ash. He spent the second war as he had spent the first. As millions of armed men tried to improve the world by killing each other, he continued to improve his world. Peaceful, regular toil in the vigorous mountain air. Frugality and, above all, serenity in the spirit had endowed this old man with awe-inspiring health. He was one of God's athletes.'

I gently blew the top of His hair. He considered His own health. Constantly tired, He felt eaten inside. No trace of purity, just insipid poison, oozing out through His every action.

'Before he had started his work the valley contained a hamlet of twelve homes and only three inhabitants; savage creatures hating one another, living physically and morally like prehistoric men. All about them nettles fed on the remains of abandoned homes. The conditions were hopeless. They waited for death.'

He thought about death frequently, no longer afraid. His brother had given him courage. He had given Him acceptance. He had given Him peace.

'Now everything was changed. The air was gentle, laden with scents, blowing with the sound like water. Neat cleanly plastered farms were a testament to happy and comfortable lives. Groves of maples, fountain pools overflowing on carpets of fresh mint. People had settled there, bringing youth, motion and the spirit of adventure. Along the roads healthy men and women, boys and girls who understood laughter, were having picnics. Someone had even planted a linden, fragrant yellowish-white flowers and heart shaped leaves, grown as an ornament, the incontestable symbol of resurrection.'

I pressed my palm on His forehead and raised my hand suddenly. Death could bring Him that. Death could bring Him resurrection.

My voice quickened. 'Over ten thousand people owed Elzeard Bouffier their happiness.'

My voice rising. 'How many people have you helped with your oppression? Elzeard helped all those people without permission, petition or thanks. How many people have you murdered with your selfish mewling?'

Voice dropping now to a whisper. I stroked His eyes once more and opened the reddening lids.

'While men died in wars he planted and regenerated the land. How many people-women-men have you sent to war? How many have you killed?'

He span.

It shattered.

I said evenly, 'Kill yourself. You are worthless. Kill yourself.'

He sat, only His face moved. A range of emotions flicked; horror, confusion, sadness, realisation, then serenity. Shards of ecstasy tore His mind. He saw His purpose. It was done.

'I am so lucky to have a friend like you! You make sense of this crazy world!' He lent across and threw his arms around his best friend. 'Thank you so much!'

'Don't mention it. One more thing, you leave from the roof of 19 St. James' Square at 11.33 in the morning on 4th of August. Have a good flight.'

6

P E R F O R M A N C E

I am a huge fan of mime. Chaplin, Lloyd, Keaton, Marceau, Tati, all fabulous and with exquisite muscle control, but I suppose it is the simplicity of illusion that attracts me.

Impossible to shift the perceived props left behind by mime artists around the world. I think of the millions of empty faux-glass boxes, the imagined balloons that can never be burst and the invisible conveyer belts conveying nothing nowhere. It would create havoc if they became real.

If Michael Jackson, when moonwalking, really did move backwards when trying to move forwards he would have had a marvellous case in his defence against any claims of his trying to get hold of minors.

'Oww! I can't get anywhere near them, your honour! Hee-hay!'

'You could always try to move backwards and in so doing move forwards toward your prey, Mr Jackson.'

'Ow! Shamone! But when I get there if I try to fiddle I end up not fiddling. And if I try not to fiddle and end up fiddling, I can't be blamed as my intention was to *not* fiddle. Quo Ed Muthafucking Demonstratum Motherfo! Hee-Hay!'

'Very clever, Mr Jackson, just like your most excellent *Thriller* music video. Case dismissed!'

Alas it is all an illusion.

A beautiful hot August day.

I was practising my mime whilst waiting for His performance. Shapes were thrown, moons walked, glass boxes erected, a little playful robotics and I leaned in unusual ways. Quite a crowd had formed and people were clapping and cheering. They wouldn't be in a minute.

There He was taking up his performance position, precisely on time, behind the crowd, ten stories up. One minute to go, and for the last thirty seconds I had been appearing to lean nonchalantly on a parking meter, in fact I was using exquisite muscle control to hold my body a few millimetres from the hot metallic surface. I stood motionless, looking up at Him. There was nervous laughter from the crowd. People, oblivious to the drama about to unfold behind them. Thirty seconds to go and I slowly unfolded my arms and pointed in His direction, still holding the apparent leaning position, putting on my best Marcel Marceau mock surprise face. The crowd turned.

I could see His dark outline. I saw His long hair billow. I could not see the expression on His face, but could feel it. I loved Him and knew Him implicitly; calm almost serene, a touch of fright brought under control with an absolute knowing of what must be done. There would be no hesitation.

At 11.33 am He threw himself forward. Arms outstretched, beckoning. The image of our last embrace flashed in my mind and His words repeated:

'I am so lucky to have a friend like you! You make sense of this crazy world!'

His hair swept back with the motion, black oil glistening in the light. Time slowed. I could see the arch of His back, that brittle sequence of bone under tension. I saw His face again, eyes widening, a tear forming at the side of one from the wind and the loss, His arms drawing closer to Himself, no one to hold. His raven hair swirled briefly in front and then quickly swept back to continue its slick. The tear, now dislodged by a jet strand, flew freely, a tiny bead of salt water straining to flow. His arms coming closer, crossing in front, and wrapping around his chest, squeezing. The motion destroying His arch, bringing His head forward in a resigned bow, knees buckled. Arms now hugging the body, legs drawn up – a falling foetus. Time slowed further. He opened, arms unfolding, back extending, legs uncoiling, defiantly facing the end, reaching to comprehend the meaning.

He hit, he returned, he rested, his hair flowed.

I felt the hot metal through the back of my shirt. His beautiful performance had broken my control and I had unconsciously allowed myself to lean back on the meter.

All the others had maintained the foetal position to impact, an instinctual reaction to extreme trauma. The brain, no longer able to cope with the surrounding environment, shuts down and ancient memory tries to protect the body from further stress. But that last defiant gesture was new. That awakening was graceful and magnificent, a noble acceptance.

'Wonderful.' I sighed. 'That was exquisite. I'm getting better. I really got to him.'

I allowed myself to descend back into anger and moonwalked over to his slightly twitching corpse. I mimed unzipping my flies, mimed urinating over his mangled form. I zipped up my imaginary fly and mimed a grotesque laugh. I took a bow. No one applauded, just sobs, gasps, impotent outrage and fear. I shrugged and performed a nice robotic sequence. Exit stage left. Still no applause, if anything, slightly more sobbing. Know your audience, I suppose.

GERRARD G. GERRARD

7

M O N E Y

And now you are judging me. You are discriminating, which is good. Keep that going, but be prepared.

It's never been a problem for me to make money. Most people have hang ups with money, but they don't address them. If they make too much they think their friends will think differently of them and that they'll become outcast.

Too little money = the same effect. So they continually swing from being broke to being almost comfortable. It is a constant struggle which serves them right. Worried about what their friends think. If your friends don't want the best for you then tell them to fuck off. Get some decent friends.

All this loyalty rubbish. *Stockholm Syndrome* everywhere, it's ridiculous. I had to disappear. The police weren't happy. There'd been too many suicides recently. All with the same memo.

Portsmouth is no stranger to suicides. Not surprising, it is a dreadful place. Spike Milligan had it consigned to Room 101 saying he hated it.

And I remember reading this in a broadsheet newspaper some years ago: '*Umm Qasr is a town similar to Southampton,*' *UK Defence Minister Geoff Hoon told the House of Commons yesterday. 'He's either never been to Southampton, or he's never been to Umm Qasr,' said one British soldier, informed of this while on patrol in Umm Qasr. Another added: 'There's no beer, no prostitutes, and people are shooting at us. It's more like Portsmouth.'*

They are wrong about the prostitutes bit. My sister was one but she never did warmongers. She was a lover not a fighter. Fabulous selection bias my sister, and a delicious sense of irony.

They'd got me in for questioning. It was my brother who had committed suicide; apparently forty people had seen me urinating on his corpse. I claimed the trauma of the situation had sent me a little mad. Terrible emotion, grief.

My lawyer, Mr Dean, was there also, as witness, and to pull me from the wreckage. Inspector Argues was laying into me. 'I don't like you or your horrible family. As far as I'm concerned the world is a better place without your thug brother. But the whole thing stinks and you, weirdo, have something to do with it.'

I had to get him off my back. I decided to do a cold reading and get him into anger. 'You know what families are like. We all have dysfunctional families.'

'Not like yours. Mother an alcoholic, sister a pro, your brother was a thug criminal, and you… you freak.'

'And what about *your* family? Look at the tension at Christmas time. Your mother berating your father, your father in apathy, watching the television not speaking –

mind
kettle
body
washing
brain
toaster
blood
floor
mother
spleen
father
bone…

'What you doing?' Shut the fuck up!'

There, at '*washing*', he flinches.

I was in. Moving around.

A twelve year-old boy watching his mother leaning on the washing machine on spin cycle, coming to a climax whilst spraying egg albumen from a turkey-baster into her own face. She turns, sweaty and exhausted and looks horrified at her son as egg white drips from her chin. That is a bit interesting.

'Your mum has a very odd fetish.'

'Shut the fuck up!'

'Turkey-baster and egg whites? Her best friend... *the washing machine?*'

'I don't know what you're talking about, you freak! Shut the fuck up.'

I had got into his mind really easily, much easier than any others before. He had gone more quickly into anger too. I was getting really good at this. Freeing my brother had released something in me. I would push this one further. I needed him to attack so I could walk free.

'Did she then make cakes with the egg whites she'd spunked over her face?'

'You fucking freak. What are you talking about?'

'In denial are we? I can see it! I'm in your mind. She made cakes and made you lot eat them.'

I laughed hysterically, mainly because I knew it would push him to strike and also because it was funny; a frustrated housewife acting out an orgy fantasy. Feeding her family cake made from imagined baby batter that had slimed from her face. What a wonderfully twisted way to make herself feel better about the prison she had created.

He launched himself across the desk and punched

me repeatedly. I let him strike and kept talking, taking him to greater depths of anger.

'And you saw her; you discovered her secret, dooming your family to a diet of real spunk. As you know, with every addiction the craving increases for harder and harder stuff, egg white wouldn't do now; she needed real jizz to get the same high. Did you ever see her collect the real stuff? Did you ever see her add it to the Victoria sponge cake mix? Laughing while stirring? Giggling while baking? Smiling, watching you and your father eat the slices, saying how delicious they were?'

The last thing I remember before losing consciousness was Inspector Argues' bloodied hands ripping the cassette out of the interview tape recorder.

I regained consciousness and my lawyer Mr Dean was waiting at the hospital bedside.

'Great act dude. You really got to him!'

'Thanks Puma. He was surprisingly easy to read. Misjudged how aggressive he would be though. How long have I been out?'

'Two days, as you predicted. Everything went as planned.' I liked my lawyer, Puma Dean. He saw things differently. He was good at his job. Something about him told me not to pry too deeply, hidden depths that man. If I got bored perhaps one day I'd have a look, but no rush. Part of me suspected that was how he was playing me. Revealing little bits of himself to keep me interested but also hinting that he wasn't that special. Fair enough. You cannot gain dominion over everyone. Not in my current level of realisation anyway.

'So, what you get?'

'You are off the suspect list. Free as a bacon sarnie in a synagogue. And a nice little compensation cheque - will take a while to come through but could be as much as four hundred large.'

'All yours, mate.'

'You sure?'

'No interest. Everything we own, owns us.'

'Yeah whatever.' Puma paused, looked curious. 'Did his mum really use real spermatozoa in the cakes or were you just twisting his lemon?'

'You saw his reaction, what do you think?'

'Argh! That's twisted!'

'Yes, but surprisingly, not that uncommon.'

And that was that. I left Portsmouth at the age of twenty. A free man.

GERRARD G. GERRARD

8

P O W E R

A nd now you are judging me. You are discriminating, which is good. Keep that going.

'With great power comes great responsibility', said some dying mug of a granddad in *Spider-Man*. What did he know? With great power comes a lot of fun and confusion. That's the thing with old people; they have all this experience, but also huge amounts of bitterness. The old begrudge the young their chance.

'Youth is wasted on the young.'

Yes, it is if all their role models are telling them to be timid and live in fear. Old people are good at surviving, that is why they are old. Survival of the fittest is such a stupid notion. Survival of the cowards. What you get is a concentration of selfish bleeders that lie. The little lies we tell ourselves get bigger with the years. Old people have whoppers. The standard pensioner has fought in two world wars, invented computing, met Gandhi in the local curry house twice, and taught Neil Armstrong what to do in the unlikely event of space rubble puncturing a hole in the command capsule - or some variation around that theme.

What is the point of old people if they can't teach the young something useful? Most pensioners cling onto life, and dwell in fear, apathy and grief. They can't bear to see anyone else succeed. Sure, they pretend to be concerned, but that's an act. They are foiling your dreams with insidious lies about life. They have spent their lives covering up the truths, and being miserable. Why should you find unlimited joy, knowledge and power? Any pensioner who doesn't embrace life fully should be encouraged to do the right thing; either cheer up and cough up some of that hard earned wisdom or shut up and free up that much needed space on public transport.

The good die young.

Old people are evil. They regret the things they didn't do. And top of the list of regrets is not having more sex, especially the women.

What kind of people are these?

Have a decent regret, not just some simple body gratification. Regret not killing your boss for being a career-cunt and making your life a misery. Regret not taking your neighbour's first born as recompense for their keeping you up with their ludicrously loud love making. Regret not finding your true self, the ultimate truth, the meaning of your existence. For fuck's sake, don't regret not having enough spunk up your vag.

The next time you visit granny in the old people's home and she gives you the sob story and you look around at all the other old people waiting for death, fearing death, do not feel sorry. They deserve it. They are responsible for all they have created around them. And it's probably all an act. As soon as you've left, feeling terrible and vowing to take her out of that beastly place, granny, having squeezed every last bit of guilt from you, is up those stairs, out of her slippers and the Aran knit cardigan and into her PVC bondage dominatrix gear, trying to make up for lost time on the sex regret by shoving butt plugs up ninety year-old retired police chief Stanley Whittering and whipping Chaz Smithers for playing with his testicles too much at tea, whilst having her tired, dried-up sniz licked out by Enid Byworthy, the ex Mayoress of Twaton.

My power was rushing, a great torrent of ability, dams breaking, energy surges. I was finding it difficult to control. It was a strange mixture of connectedness with everything and also a terrible anger raging. The fluctuating extremes are under control now and I am at peace but in those days it was carnage.

I decided to go for a mass suicide attempt. Push the boundaries. Single people were easy, but could I get a crowd to give up the ghost?

I had travelled to London to study people, to really immerse myself in the flow of life.

'When a man is tired of London he is tired of life,' said Dr Samuel Johnson, thus contributing to the suicide rate in that city. I would continue his good work.

Dr Sam suffered from scrofula as a kid and so had a horribly scarred face. He also was hard of hearing, had poor eyesight and displayed numerous tics and involuntary movements. His Scottish friend James Boswell suggested he had *Tourettes*, and that in some way explains his obsession with the dictionary; keen to get all those swear words into official parlance and so make himself less offensive to the well-educated gentry. It is encouraging that 18th Century England would allow an ugly, compulsive, overweight Touretto to help generations of people form religious and moral opinions.

What do we have today? Boris Johnson?

Plus ça change…

GERRARD G. GERRARD

9

J O B S

I was working in a local government office in Hackney. Welfare and Finance Officer. It was the only thing *Manpower* had on its books. Welfare and Finance meant debt collecting. Collecting rent from the late paying tenants in council-run tower block slums. Drug addicts, prostitutes, senile geriatrics, and art students. It was a fantastic job. I could practise to my heart's content and no one would notice. And in the process I'd get some money back for the council. Everyone's a winner.

I wanted to experience commuting so took up lodgings in the town of Chelmsford, Essex. And that was when I formulated the idea. I noticed patterns and rhythms. People would stand at the same place on the platform, sit on the same seat, and talk to the same people, forming cliques. If I could infiltrate those cliques I was in with a chance of precipitating a mass suicide event.

Morning commutes fall into three phases; the Early Bird, the Mong-Artiste and the Middle Manager.

The Early Bird group gets to work at 6.45 am and consists of the minions of mammon; the financial traders who haven't quite made it and are still struggling to get any edge they can. The successful traders are being limousined or helicoptered into work an hour later. Also in this group are the shift workers in IT, builders and sanitation engineers. This group is bleary-eyed and polite. These are people who keep themselves to themselves, if bumped they apologise. They are trying to make the best of a bad situation and are too saddled with debt to think straight and move to a better environment. How can you feel compassion for this group of idiots? Strangely in those days I did, a little.

The Mong-Artistes get to work anytime after 9 am, and are either too thick to have responsible jobs and so serve in fast food joints or chemists, or they are artists working to support themselves whilst pursuing more worthwhile projects. I felt something for this group, what was it? Pity. Pity with a pinch of contempt.

The Middle Managers are the career-cunts. They arrive at work at 8.15 am. They have titles like 'Executive Under-Manager Procuring Department' or 'Intermediate B2B Vice President'. They've made it their business to bring misery to most people. They are intelligent enough to work a spread sheet or gain an *Open University* MBA but not so bright as to realise the futility of it all. They take absolutely no responsibility and are experts in blaming. They are business bullies and should be destroyed. I decided to release the Middle Managers from their perdition. It was a bit of work, but worth it. I would set the alarm for 5.30 am and drive north east to Clacton to catch the 6.34 am back into London Liverpool Street, arriving at what I playfully termed 'cunt o'clock' or six minutes past eight. This train provided the biggest bang for the buck as it called at the most stations allowing maximum infiltration of cliques.

Clacton - 6.34 am
I would board the train and sit with Margret 'You Couldn't Make It Up' Spendol and her three cronies. Margret was your classic fat, sour woman several years into the menopause who thought everyone fancied her and that all men are rapists. She was surrounded by three thin sycophantic fifty year-olds desperate for a bit of that rancidly hormonal clunge. She was very easy to tip over the edge. I

would sit with this group for twenty-eight minutes, gently plant the scripts then get off at Colchester and move into the next carriage.

Colchester - 7.02 am

Tom would be waiting eagerly for his morning spirituals. Thomas 'Wassup!' Branchard was an aspiring young accountant, eager for promotion and to get to the top. He would be my main weapon. I would sit and provide him with human behavioural nuggets that he could use against his contemporaries, all the while planting the 'Master of the Universe' script. I only had ten minutes with Tom but he was young and learnt quickly and I had set aside several months for the induction of this train.

Kelvedon - 7.13 am

I'd move to the next carriage at Kelvedon. Vivien 'Any Popular Catchphrase From A Third Rate Comedy Show' Swain would great me with her sarcastic 'Soon be the weekend, mustn't grumble' routine. Dreadful woman, and so the 'Judge Dread' script seemed appropriate.

Witham - 7.18 am

Rick 'Not Bad For A Tuesday' Wangfoot. Compliance officer. Enough said.

Chelmsford - 7.27 am

Andy 'What A Cunt' Wilkins. Out of all of them I couldn't wait for him to die the most. Several times I contemplated taking him aside and having a quiet word, but I had put a lot of work into this already and didn't want to start again. I had planned a particularly nasty 'Fire God' script for him, by way of compensation. The eleven minutes with him felt like several lifetimes. He was the most repellently self-obsessed man I have ever met. He was so blinkered to the joy and abundance around him, just driven by the goal to be the King of Kunts. Toss bag was too nice a description for him. He was the bag that the toss bags used to toss into. The Wanker's wanker. On the plus side, he would, on a daily basis, increase my conviction that I was doing humanity a great favour.

Shenfield - 7.38 am
Sharon 'You Staring At My Tits' Florez. All cleavage, strong napalm perfume and badly applied foundation, Ms Florez was your classic sex career-cunt. She would sleep with the people above, flirt with the people below and have HR take out the competition with sexual harassment claims. The 'Rabbit' script was too good for her.

Stratford - 7.55 am – 8.06 am
Driver. I'd get off at Stratford and have a word with the driver in to Liverpool Street. I really grew to like Martin, a shame he was soon to die. Collateral damage though, it was what he would have wanted. He understood the plan and was happy to die a martyr. There would be other good eggs on the train I knew. People who got up late that morning, or ones that were seeing the light and mending their ways gradually. But I calculated it was about five percent, and perfectly acceptable for an operation of this type. If I'd had the time I'd have persuaded them it was for the best. But I had already spent over three months on this production and that fucking Andy Wilkins was really getting to me.

10

T R A I N

I was ready; the train was ready after three months, three weeks and three days of preparation. I boarded at 6.34 am carrying my bag of goodies. I gave Margret her 'present' and sat silently as she contemplated its significance. I left the train at 7.02 am, uttering the command:

'Marge, it will soon be time to cut loose.'

I entered the next carriage, gave Thomas his 'present' and sat silently until Kelvedon. I gave his command as I left:

'Tom, it will soon be time to spray.'

The next carriage. Vivien stared at her 'present' as I sat silently.

'Vivien, it will soon be time to judge.'

I left.

At Whitham Rick brooded over the 'present'. Again I sat silently, then:

'Rick, it will soon be time to comply fully.'

Chelmsford, and Andy sat motionless, meditating on his coming performance. I sat silently finally enjoying his company.

'Andy, it will soon be time to shine.'

As I entered the next carriage at Shenfield the train went into lock down. All alarms were disabled, and doors locked by the driver Martin. Good man. I sat silently with Sharon, her 'present' resting on her lap.

'Sharon, it will soon be time to give everyone love.'

I got up and knocked on the driver's door. Martin let me in. I took control of the intercom.

'Ladies and gentlemen. We shall be arriving a little earlier than expected at London Liverpool Street. Please make sure you leave all your baggage behind you.'

'Marge - cut loose!'

'Tom - squeeze!'

'Vivien - judge!'

'Rick - comply!'

'Andy - shine!'

'Sharon - love!'

'The rest you of you enjoy the show!'

I could hear the gasps of astonishment from the carriage next door, and feel the mayhem being created in the other carriages.

Ten minutes until Liverpool Street. I left the train by the driver's door. I had instructed him to pull away slowly so I could survey my handy work as the train went by.

I caught glimpses of the carnage in full flow as the train pulled out of the station.

Sharon was standing on the seats in First Class pleasuring herself with the large rabbit dildo I had presented to her earlier, surrounded by astonished commuters. Some commuters were bravely trying to ignore her by reading the *Daily Mail*; others had got up and moved to standard class, tutting, and drawing attention to her show. A couple of late builders were egging her on with shouts of 'Go on, love!' through the glass partition. Good lads. Collateral damage though. They'd understand. Collateral damage; good enough for governments, good enough for me. Sharon was providing excellent misdirection for Tom who was working his way through the carriages mopping up any survivors. I could imagine Tom, moments later, bursting through the door and spraying the carriage with bullets from the *Uzi*, and Sharon releasing the sarin gas as she climaxed.

The next carriage was in a state of confusion. People wondering why the doors hadn't opened at Stratford and what all the fuss was in the adjoining carriages. The third carriage came by and there was Tom gently squeezing the trigger in short bursts. Not as much panic as you might expect. It was almost peaceful. Surprised looks and then death.

The next carriage was quiet, but gently catching fire. Tom had caught up with Andy who had managed to walk through two carriages before collapsing. Good effort considering he had dowsed himself in petrol and disobeyed the **NO SMOKING** signs by lighting up a cheeky *Silk Cut*.

The next was starting to flame nicely, bullet-riddled bodies twisted in panic. Quiet.

Then Andy's carriage, several burning bodies caught by the fireball effect of lighting petrol in a confined space, burning gently and dripping fat. A smoke-stained hand appeared at the window briefly then fell away.

Those who are possessed by nothing possess everything.

GERRARD G. GERRARD

11

G L I T C H

Rick came into view, typical bloody compliance officer, missing the point completely. If it wasn't for the enthusiasm of Tom's trigger finger there might have been survivors. Rick was supposed to take the *Remington 870* pump action shotgun and follow Tom, to ride shotgun with him. It was my way of injecting a subtle bit of humour into the whole grisly affair, something for the more intelligent passengers to pick up on and be rewarded by, before being dispatched. But Rick had gone straight to his end program and blown his own head off at the start. He was sitting with the shotgun held between his knees, hands on trigger and barrel, what little remained of his head effecting a considered expression. I imagined it was just the sort of pose he would strike in all those futile meetings he organised.

In death as in life, like a suit and a tie; he was pointless.

He had really upset me initially. But now I've learnt to look for the perfection where the seeming imperfection seems to be. And I realise he was like a monument to the whole purpose of the mass suicide performance. He was the statue in the middle of the carnage to remind me and anyone else who cared that this is what the commuter train stood for. I load of bereft people mindlessly going about their jobs, oblivious to the abundance that surrounded them. But, as I said at the time, I was enraged. I barely registered the remainder of the performance and can only imagine what great things Marge did with her slim *Laguiole* carving knife or Vivien's gusto with the lump hammer.

In those days I was filled with anger and pride and Rick, that little compliance scrotum, had ruined my masterpiece. In those days nothing could lift me from the depression except the *Samaritans*.

I stormed out of Stratford and straight to the nearest pay phone. I called the *Samaritans* and asked for Dave, my current do-gooder. I'd been grooming him for weeks and he was ready to go.

'Hello, Dave?'

'Yes, is that you, Mister Mann?'

'Yes. I've had a bad day, Dave.'

'Do you want to talk about it?'

'Yes. Are you sitting comfortably? I shall begin.'

Dave shifted.

'It's been a bad day, Dave, a really bad day. What's the point of it all?'

Dave remained silent. His mind stirred.

'No one understands me, Dave. Do you know how that feels?'

'Yes.'

'You try your best, Dave, to create something special and it gets ruined. Have you ever felt like that, Dave?'

'Yes.'

'A meticulous plan, ruined by the one who doesn't care. Do you know someone like that, Dave, someone in the past?'

'Yes.'

'Destroyed. All your hopes… '

And that was as far as I was able to get before I heard him place the phone on his desk, walk to the window and open it.

Concerned voices:

'What are you doing, Dave?'

'Dave?'

Then the familiar gasp.

Fuck that was quick.

Usually I'd have to go through the whole 'shattered - pity - depression - grief - apathy - self destruct' spiral before that would happen. Usually a good thirty minutes phone work. That really cheered me up.

A new personal best.

GERRARD G. GERRARD

12

G R A T I F I C A T I O N

And so you judge me. You are discriminating, which is good. Keep that.

My *Samaritans* fetish attracted them to me. The Xaja, they came. I remember I was indulging my body with Monica. Exercise, eating and sex, all the same thing essentially. Simple physical gratification, keeping the body satisfied. And this is where most people make the mistake. The point is to satisfy the body to stop it nagging so you can free yourself to pursue more worthwhile things. People let the mind get involved. The mind is a servant, the body a simple tool.

You are a master, *the* Master.

The mind tells you that the food could be better, you should exercise more and the sex was fabulous.

Or the opposite. Or an infinite variation on the theme. Wrong.

And so people get distracted by the pursuit of beauty and perfection. This trivial distraction is the scourge of humanity. The truth is that everything is perfect.

I realised from an early age that fat birds were a much better shag than slim supposedly prettier ones. They're more willing to let go of inhibition, the big girls, and often grateful for the attention. But I also realised there was more. You could extrapolate the phenomenon. Pretty girls use their minds too much. They are concerned with external effects. That is where their power base is. The image they present to the world, one of subtle demure beauty or stunning visuals.

They get really self-conscious when this normal power base is disrupted and there is an image change of say a cock shoved roughly into their mouths. Sure, they might get excited and a little surprised but it's not too long before the program of image takes over and restricts the body from really getting into it. Same goes for fat and ugly girls but to a lesser extent.

I used to experiment before settling on my preference. Midgets were fun but dwarves were better. Deaf girls were sensational, especially ugly deaf girls. To hear them howl is still a delight. Absolutely no mind monitor in place to alter the noise. So what you get is a very deep, instinctual animal resonance, whether it is from pleasure or pain. Exquisite.

I experimented with my ability to alter the mind, to get rid of it completely and so get a true body response. But there was always something left; a shadow of mind, meddling, tingeing the response with an impurity. And that tiny impurity was amplified in my mind because it was a reflection of my craft. Oh, that pride again, holding me back. That's the big one for most people.

I dabbled with the mentally retarded. Not a good idea but interesting nonetheless. I should have known better but curiosity got the better of me. Don't get me wrong, they were much better than the able-minded, more pure and instinctual but the mind was always there, chaotic, free reign, unpredictable. Annoying. Marvellous cuddles though. I'll miss those.

In the end I realised what any forty year-old woman with cats knows; that you cannot beat a really good wank. Not the usual western standard wank, riddled with learned guilt and disapproval, but an honest-to-goodness proper wank, like a really good dump clear-out after a particularly satisfying curry.

So there I was with Monica, my right-hand woman. I had tried to be a homosexual wanker with Quentin, but he never really did it for me. Susan the Trannywank was good, but not as good as Monica, I could really give myself to her, really let go. She was wearing a lovely floral print hand dress (a modified gardening glove), and I had applied make-up to her finger/thumb mouth. She was blowing me like a raspberry, and I was losing control. Marvellous rhythm, perfect grip – she knew how I liked it. She had thrown me against the wall for the third time, banging my head with her roughness, I forgave her instantly, I admired her passion. Getting to my vinegar strokes, Monica urging me on, my mind out of the way, my body letting go, my self looking on detached and amused and... in they burst.

I stopped abruptly, their attention focused on the glove puppet and my engorged member.

'Mister Mann, come with us. Do not resist.'

'I will come with my self. LEAVE now and let me finish.'

I had perfected the Voice by this stage and could usually get my way. The perfect pitch to make a person do my will. Simple commands like LEAVE, GO, JUMP. These people just stood there. It wasn't working on them, but I knew I could have them in a fight and so decided to take them apart. They were good; it took a bit longer than expected. But soon they were all down, unconscious and tied up, three men and one woman.

I finished my lovemaking by coming in the weak one's face. He had flinched when I used the Voice, if it wasn't for the others he would have run. They were all strong, as good as Stan at fighting, the woman was actually better.

I wiped my cock in her hair.

GERRARD G. GERRARD

13

D Y I N G

And so you judge me, you are discriminating, which is good. We are the same. You are me.

Everything you own, owns you. Fear the man who has nothing to lose.

I hadn't been attacked for a while. In the past I would simply immobilise those who tried and then persuade them to take their own lives. Violence is not the way and so the lost souls needed to be shown. I wasn't going to kill these yet, they intrigued me.

I had dislocated all their arms and legs, and had rubbed the ball joints into the sockets. The pain would usually make most talk, or faint − it is a delicate balance. These guys were good, excellent control. Not a whimper. I moved to the eyes, popping one out in each of them and showing them an extended view of the room and my smiling face. Same result. Not a murmur. Hard as nails.

The skill with torture is to get increasingly intimate. Start with the basics and then go more psychological. Introduce them slowly to their deepest program, their deepest fear; the fear of dying.

Pain and dying are very different. Pain merely hints at death, only scratches the surface, it's an *amuse-gueule* in the banquet of life. Fear of Death is the main course.

I had lost my fear of death at the age of ten. The best present he had given me. I love that brother of mine. The beatings had reached an obscene point; random, vicious and frequent. He took my manhood with every session, making me retreat further. I was a loner, not interested in the usual joys of childhood. Instead of socialising with others, laughing, running, I played with my chemistry set and microscope, collecting insects to study and persecute, vainly trying to get control. Ridiculed by the others, especially him, I decided to exercise the only real control any of us has. Control over ourselves.

I stood on the ledge and contemplated ending my life, exercising control by making a commitment to end the suffering. I looked at my tiny child feet, then the red and black pattern of the tiled driveway below, wondering if I was high enough for my head to smash fully open on that hard surface. I remembered skateboarding on those tiles, and the noise the loose ones made as the wheels rolled over them. There was some give in that surface, was it hard enough? Should I go and find somewhere higher, surrounded by concrete – the *Tricorn Centre* car park would be ideal, a beautiful bit of sixties brutalism. If I jumped up and quickly entered into a dive, would I gain enough speed to spill my brains, snap my neck, and crush my spine – die of the trauma? Or would I end up in a wheelchair a vegetable? Or a trapped mind in a useless body? Perhaps I should climb on the roof and make sure. Decisions, decisions. And then it occurred to me, I wasn't afraid at that moment to die. It was just a decision. And I was making a meal of it. I laughed properly for the first time. Life did not matter. Wonderful laughter. Death did not matter. Beautiful, rich, deep laughter.

Then my fear came back. I didn't want to die anymore. I wanted to get back inside. My legs started to shake and I felt dizzy. I climbed back in to safety.

My brother continued to condition me over the

coming years. The want of death would come. I'd go to my favourite place, that first floor window ledge, and contemplate my demise. This occurred frequently until I was free of the fear of death and no longer needed that special place. Thanks brother, what a gift!

Most people are not lucky enough to have a brother like mine and so fear death. And I suspected these people that had interrupted my intimate moment with Monica were further advanced down the path of enlightenment, but still feared death. I just had to find that trigger and then I'd own them fully.

The woman wanted to talk. Not because she was afraid. She soon would be. She was sitting in a pile of her own excrement, most joints dislocated, one eye resting on her cheek, spunk in her hair, and all with exquisite control. No trace of fear. But she knew I could make her talk and she was just cutting to the chase.

I felt compassion. I wanted to show her the fear and then help her overcome it. But her-indoors, Monica, didn't. Best not upset the little woman, she's the boss.

I took the weakest one. There I went again, trying to help the underdog. Give him an experience the others haven't had. Maybe he could figure it out himself. Maybe he'd die trying.

I made him comfortable, popping his extremities back in. I got him a cushion. I offered him a cup of tea. He didn't want one. I stood behind him and massaged his neck, then his bruised head. I started to talk. And talk.

And talk.

Talk.

They had been programmed well. I soothed and talked, and massaged, stroked, talked, and comforted. It took me the best part of an hour. As a guide my average time for a person to go from happiness to suicide in those days was around five minutes. These guys were hard.

But finally he cracked. There – I found the chink, and I was so excited by the challenge I steamed in full force. His scream was fabulous. What a release! What fear! Tears rolling down his cheeks, veins rising in his temples, red-faced he screamed and screamed. I talked and soothed, and cajoled, stroked his brow to help him through. He screamed from ancient times, primitive. I soothed. He peaked. Almost there. I soothed. He burst. I lost him. Almost.

He died. Ah well.

I kissed his sweaty, cum-stained brow and while closing his eyelids thanked him for allowing me the chance to help him.

I turned excitedly to the others.

'That was fantastic! Who's next?'

They started to talk.

14

X A J A

The media had done a very good cover up of the carnage I'd created at Liverpool Street Station that foggy autumn morning. They'd got the call from that special governmental department that gives the orders for propaganda. The media complied and blamed leaves on the line for the delays. Or was it points? Or signals? Two trains crashing? Doesn't matter, the few people affected by the carnage promptly tutted and got on with their mundane lives, or created lies about what they had seen, it gave them something to focus on, to briefly lift them into something of importance. The 'I was there when John Kennedy died' effect. Were you bollocks.

The incident had alerted the XAJA and their forensics combed the burnt wreck for anything significant. Shotgun, *Uzi*, lump hammer, carving knife, canister of petrol and an XXL rabbit vibrator. Not the usual haul from your average train crash.

There were no clues linking it to me. CCTV was not popular in those days, and the ones around were clunky, obvious and easy to avoid. No survivors and no one interviewed at Stratford could identify me (I practically invented the hoody), but my *Samaritan* fetish linked me. The lines are tapped, calls recorded and sixty volunteers jumping out of windows, blowing their brains out, overdosing, or killing their co-workers over the course of five years doesn't go unnoticed. Mister Li apparently had this ability to far sense. I was an anomaly in the fabric of existence and all he had to do was watch and wait and I would reveal myself. I suppose the Hackney council flats suicide rate spike didn't help either. On reflection I was a bit tortured in those days and was crying out for attention. I take full responsibility for what happens to me always, and I am to blame for bringing them to me. I was calling.

It was explained to me that XAJA was a name conjured up by a government spook called Mister Li. It was Ajax spelt backwards. Ajax was an ancient Greek warrior who committed suicide. In Homer's *The Iliad*, he is described as of great stature and colossal frame, the tallest and strongest of all the Achaeans. When Achilles dies, killed by Paris (and that meddling god Apollo), Ajax and Odysseus take on the Trojans, get the body back and bury it next to his best mucker, Patroclus. Ajax, with his fuck off hammer, manages to beat the crap out of the Trojans, while Odysseus nabs the corpse and rides off in his chariot. After the burial, both heroes want the armour, because what is the point of going to all that effort for a pat on the back? But after some discussion, Odysseus is given the armour. Ajax is furious, really pissed off and not surprisingly as he did most of the donkey work while the favoured pretty boy ponced around in his wide boy wheels. Ajax, exhausted, passes out. Athena then puts a spell on him and when he wakes up he goes off and slaughters a flock of sheep, thinking that they are the Achaean leaders, including Odysseus and Agamemnon. He comes to his senses, covered in blood, realises what he's done, loses face with his crew and decides he'd prefer to kill himself rather than live in shame. He committed suicide with Hector's sword. Idiot.

So this spy, Mister Li, runs a department of psychological assassins called the XAJA, named after a Homeric warrior who committed suicide. What a pretentious cunt. I invited him round for tea.

15

T E A

A man never forgets the sight of his first spunk bubble. I was eight and it was Tony White's bubble.

Tony was one of those blokes that matured very early; either a genetic throwback or a precursor of what's to come. Judging by his thick brow, long arms and difficulty with multi-syllabic words, I suspected he was a throwback.

We were rummaging around the local tip, a piece of waste land near to Canoe Lake, Southsea. We had just found a bag of seventies pornography and had retired to the derelict garages to have a proper look. I was intrigued by the six girl pile-up centre spread of a *Razzle* and wondered why the title read 'Block of Flaps', when Tony shouted, 'Oi! Man! Look!'

I turned and there was Tony standing with his extraordinary thick cock in his hand. Like two veiny cans of Coke laid end to end. He wasn't a proper eight year-old, more like a dwarf with a big red penis. He was a freak.

'What the fuck have you been looking at to grow a thing like that?'

'A *wo*-man. Hairy.' And he holds up a full page picture of an enormous, hairy beaver. I have never seen such an intimidating vagina in my life. This thing was bellicose. It was growling. Snarling. A cross between Brian Blessed sneezing and a tarantula crushed with a cricket bat. It made me shrink, but it inflamed Tony, further proof he was a caveman in disguise. 'Man! Look! Bubble!'

I looked again and there it was, glistening in the half

light. Swirling patterns as the fluid strained under tension, white in places, then opaque, a rippling oil slick of protein. His cock had produced a bubble. That pearly lustre, beautiful colours like an abalone shell, the wings of a bird or the carapace of an exotic insect. Flowing patches of colour slicking on an oily street after a rain shower. Red turning to blue-green reflections, the skin of the bubble glistening with complementary colours. As the skin thins, blue appears then magenta and so on to yellows. The yellow fades and darkness threatens, black is coming and the undeniable burst. But then fresh material is provided like a fluvial tide and the colours reverse. Pulsating in a chaotic rhythm. Mesmerising, white spirals into blues and pinks. Ordered bands appear, restoring the structure. Red to blue to violet and more yellows appear and then darkness threatens, again. A fresh bloom and the colour restores, the bubble increases in size and the majesty of iridescence blossoms.

I am taken to a field of many coloured flowers swaying in a summer breeze. The field spins and the flowers blend, white appears. The field spins slows and the individual flower colours weave again. And so the pulse goes on.

I am transfixed by the simple beauty, the quivering bubble, the fragility of its life. A stray breeze, a sudden impact, a mote of dust could at any moment end its life. But still it breathes, oblivious to the dangers, reaching for life, straining to grow, increasing the danger of extinction with every new burst of energy. But the colours surge, bright greens and blues, it is strong and it appears as a vibrant planet. It grows more substantial and I gently descend to its surface. As I get closer I begin to make out detail; not the manmade structures of roads, temples or cities, nor the natural structures of mountains, forests and oceans, but a forever evolving, morphing landscape offering delights momentarily and then fading to further delights. This is beyond the body, beyond the mind, on the cusp of creation – the zone before creation. I push further and see the other side, briefly, just a glimpse. What is it? – my mind tries to comprehend. The mind is imperfect and of no use here. I push it away, and try to glimpse again. Too late, I cannot control and begin to rise above the world and see the colour swirl again. The planet is bigger and growing. The colours are fading; the vibrant greens have been replaced with insipid yellows. Darkness approaches and the inevitable burst. Red, blue, green, yellow turns to black and - pop! Tony's bubble bursts, he stands grinning, lightly stroking his slimy bulb and I am cursed forever.

Any bubble I see now reminds me of the eight year-old, dwarf caveman Tony White and his enormous spunk-bubble-producing knob.

I stirred the tea and watched the bubble of milk dance across the surface. I laughed. Mister Li sat on my couch, immovable.

'Why do you laugh?'

'You tell me, Mister Psychology.'

'Tony White's Spunk Bubble?'

How the fuck?

He was good.

16

L U S T

And so he had me. We should strive to attain no desire. As long as there is want, we lack, and are trapped in a world of limitation. Desire is the great enemy of abundant joy. But that was a fucking awesome trick and I wanted to know how he did it. I desired the ability to do it myself. It may be his only trick but it was magnificent.

My mind raced. Was it just extreme information gathering? Perhaps Tony White was not an eight year-old with a big fat Neanderthal cock as my memory had told me, but a notorious dwarf paedophile with a seventies porn fetish who wanted to get into my knickers. Was he on a register and this Mister Li had done his homework and extrapolated, got his computers to help? Had I spoken about this before?

No.

That was mindreading pure and simple. I had seen it in my own craft, but mine was more amorphous, more intuitive. This was something new. This was direct.

I tested.

'Good. And what did he say after the bubble burst?'

Li paused, looked, relaxed. Looked past me as when one enters combat. He smiled.

'Muff. Hairy. Mmmmm muff.' With almost the exact accent Tony'd used, deep, staccato and rasping.

'OK, so you have this trick to offer. What do you want from me in return?'

'A special job. You will enjoy it.'

I didn't like Mister Li. He was impenetrable. No

surface to get hold of. Just as well because in those days I would have torn him apart. The slightest weakness shown and I would have had him. He was possibly the most repellent individual I had ever met; an abomination, abhorred by nature. He annoyed me, intensely. I used to plan exquisite deaths and lessons for him, but only after he had given me that secret. He knew that. We are radio receivers and transmitters. If you think a thing about a person you might as well tell him. A person knows what you think about him, if he is brave enough to look.

I love him now of course, in my own special way, in the way of the Ultimate Truth.

He could read me but I couldn't read him. He sat on my sofa knowing he wasn't seconds away from death. I didn't know he wasn't seconds away from death. I thought I was going to kill him. Then I thought I would let him live until I had that secret. But then he had given me clues as to how it was done, I could work on it, kill him. I was debating for some time. But he knew he wasn't going to die that day. He did know he would die someday. I wonder if he knew how and when I was eventually going to kill him. He frustrated me, I wanted to harm him, to get rid of him, to get some reaction from him but I knew it would do no good. Not yet. I moved across the room to the radiator. I punched the Xaja that was handcuffed to it.

'What are you going to do with them?'

'Let them go.'

'Why don't you free them?'

'Those two would die. The woman stands a chance. Do you want to be free, love?'

She did. But she was afraid. Not a good start.

'When did you begin their training?'

'They were sixteen.'

'Too old I suspect. But she's tough. I could go a little more gently. Not get so carried away. Best she gets patched up first. You? Do you want to be free?'

'How do you know I am not?'

'I know.'

He flinched, very slight pride. Got him. I could work on that, it would take time, barely perceptible. How does he control it? Another trick that could be useful. It could wait. But he was still right that I wouldn't kill him now.

He must die.

GERRARD G. GERRARD

17

E S T A B L I S H M E N T

L ooking back, I wasn't free. I was freer than most but not completely free.

My nemesis, Mister Li, taught me so much.

Thank the people who annoy you.

He was reflecting my faults. I was stuck in pride.

I had a wooden display cabinet in my downstairs loo, an amusing little thing that my dinner party guests would comment on. It measured thirty centimetres by fifteen centimetres. Inside were little shields, like the ones posh people mount game hunting trophies on; the heads of lions, deer, antelope and tigers. Mine had insect heads. Underneath the shields were the common and family names of each specimen, the date and the place where the beast was killed, and finally the weapon used. Magnifying glasses were in front of the specimens to enlarge the words and the features.

Ten specimens in all:

Ant - Formicidae - 1984 - The Patio - Kettle
Wasp - Vespidae - 1975 - Window - Daily Mail
Bee - Andrenidae - 1972 - Flower bed - Smoke and lethal injection
Fly - Brachycera - 1979 - Sandwich - 2 slices of bread
Dragonfly - Aeshnidae - 1982 - Pond - Drowning
Moth - Drepanidae - 1981 - Wardrobe - Dry cleaning
Earwig - Forficulidae - 1971 - Park - Andy's face
Butterfly - Nymphalidae - 1984 - Garden - Secateurs
Grasshopper - Acrididae - 2010 - Living room - Strangled
Beetle - Noteridae - 1981 - Patio - Magnifying glass

And this...

'Something in the insect seems to be alien to the habits, morals, and psychology of this world, as if it had come from some other planet: more monstrous, more energetic, more insensate, more atrocious, more infernal than our own.'

— **Maurice Maeterlinck (1862–1949)**

The *Noteridae* beetle in the display case was in fact a *Dytiscidae* as it didn't have the distinctive noterid platform underneath in the form of a plate between the second and third pair of legs. Anyone who failed to notice this would be targeted for 'correction'. Not surprisingly, no one ever noticed. It was made all the more difficult by the fact that only the heads were on display. Just my little joke.

And so my guests thought it was an ironic piece designed to provoke. They'd comment on the lunacy of pretending to be brave, of shooting a tiger from the safety of an elephant or *Land Rover*, of killing the beautiful wild animals of the Savannah. But the point of the piece was a little more pertinent than that. Mammals encompass some five thousand four hundred species, including humans. Insects are the most diverse group of animals on the Earth, with over a million described species and estimates of a further thirty million un-described species, representing over ninety percent of the life forms on the planet. There are more dragonfly species than different types of mammal. The first true mammal appeared on the Earth about one hundred and fifty million years ago with *Homo Sapiens* -Modern Humans - appearing one hundred and thirty thousand years ago. The insects have been around for four hundred million years; over twice as long as the earliest mammal and two thousand six hundred and sixty-six point six six six times longer than humans.

To understand the success of insects is to appreciate our own failures. Humans only notice the superficial. The average mind is closed to detail. The insects own this planet, a planet more monstrous, more energetic, more insensate, more atrocious and more infernal than the planet the average human perceives. The purpose of the cabinet was to alert viewers to this fact, to open their minds to a more pressing reality, that humans make no difference to the planet.

Mister Li was playing at being in charge of the planet, involved in some secret world group. Conspiracy theories abound about the Illuminati, Bilderberg Group, Freemasons, New World Order, The Babylonian Brotherhood or WhateverTheFuckCuntatti. Each has its own elements of truth. But all these theories are essentially futile. As was the organisation for which Mister Li worked.

Mister Li initially wanted me to train the XAJA. I started with the strong woman from the flat, Carla. She survived but had no intention of coming back. And that was the problem. It was easy to take them higher but they had no desire to come back. Once they had the realisation, what was the point of continuing in the grossest state possible for a being? They had no desire to inhabit the limited mind and body; that urine, faeces, slime and bile-producing body, that irrational, paranoid, warped and impure mind. Only the really sick come back. And they eventually die from the madness.

I managed to free ten of them before they stopped the project. I still speak to them. They are around me now, my friends, calling me to join them.

But I can't. I have things to do.

GERRARD G. GERRARD

18

R E L I G I O N S

The Order decided to use my talents for the problem the Xaja, trained but released by me, were supposed to tackle. I decided to play along. I was learning from them too.

The problem was simple enough. One of the tools they used for controlling the masses was starting to get a little too arrogant. They could sense a push for more power; a concerted effort between the various factions to raise awareness of religion and so gain more support. More wars than usual breaking out. War is a crude but very effective way to get the average human believing in God. Perverse but true. 'Would God let these things happen, these atrocities: murder, rape, genocide? No there must be another reason. Oh, I don't like to think about the detail, shelve responsibility and start to pray. If I am faithful enough He will explain!'

The problem was upsetting the balance of the Order and they wanted to send it a couple of messages. The idea being that the Xaja would infiltrate the various religions, befriend the leaders of these religions and then program them to commit suicide at a certain time. The event would be hushed up by the media as they controlled that too, but the religions and the heads of media would have been sent a very clear message to behave themselves, take the money and the live the good life. Apparently, this flux occurred repeatedly every couple of hundred years, but remedying it had got more difficult as the human population increased. This was deemed the right mixture of psychology and brutality. 'We can kill you in more ways than you can imagine and with panache.'

It took the average Xaja four months to program a religious leader. And the shelf life of the instruction was limited to a couple of days. There are over one thousand major religions in the world and they wanted to send a message to all of them, so they needed one thousand Xaja. They only had fifty trained agents so far and I had killed thirty of those. But I didn't tell them about the ones I had freed. They didn't have the resources or the time.

It was observed that the train crash I had caused was a work of assassination art. There were no survivors. I had initially assumed that the fervour of the inducted ones had taken care of that, but it was pointed out that statistically there should have been a few survivors on a train of that size. It was as if, over the course of those months, I had infused the rest of the travellers with a sense of hopelessness. My presence had affected everyone, not just the inducted. Usually there would be some miracle story of a bullet-ridden woman clinging on to life and eventually pulling through because she dreamed of her loved ones calling her back. But it seemed I had infused everyone with the desire to let go of the futility of their existence.

Must have been the way I looked at people. Now that was a power I could work on.

I liked religion, some marvellous ideas, enormous paradoxes, delicious ironies, and really warped stories. So I accepted the mission.

The Bible is actually my favourite book. I always carry a copy. I used to have doubts about some of the things I did, but a quick read of Deuteronomy or Leviticus and I'm back on track.

The sixth commandment - Thou shall not kill - used to puzzle me. The first commandment - Thou shall have no other gods before me - if broken, is punishable by death, either by stoning *(Deuteronomy 17:1-5)* or damnation *(Mark 16:16)* or utter destruction *(Exodus 22:20)*. But the sixth commandment says you are not allowed to do that, so in doing the Lord's work you must die too. It used to puzzle me, but now I appreciate it for the fabulous piece of mind-fucking that it is. That is a proper God; lay down a few hardcore rules, chuck in as many paradoxes and see what happens. Fucking first class inspiration. No wonder Christianity, Islam and Judaism have so many curious followers.

The Koran, Tanakh, The Vedas, The Pali Canon, Shinto Scriptures, Dasam Granth, Kitáb-i-Aqdas and writings from the twenty-four Tirthankaras have all been inspirations to me, but *The Bible* was the book that kept me going through the dark times.

I am not antireligious. People who are antireligious see religions as dangerous, destructive, divisive, foolish and absurd. As do I. And that is why I am pro-religion.

I really do not like atheists, secular humanists and the antireligious. They have no imagination. Religious stories are wonderful, passionate, paradoxical, warped, sick, disturbing. They make you think 'WOW!'

Secular stories are so dull: 'There is this big universe and it is getting bigger, but one day it will stop getting bigger and start to get smaller and crush everything and then start again, and we are here because err... Did we tell you about 'survival of the fittest' yet?' These stories make you think 'WANK!'

Of all the contracts to date this was going to be the most

professionally satisfying. I had orchestrated many seemingly impossible assassinations and now they were asking for a very special event; a mass hypnosis and suicide show. They didn't think it was possible but they asked nevertheless. I assured them it could be done.

Once the initial creative thinking and necessary inductions had been done this was going to be simple. The subjects were very compliant, easy to manipulate and control. Clerics and preachers. Holy men. Sheep.

The useful thing about the religious is that most of the really utilitarian hypnotic scripts have already been firmly, deeply implanted by their theological teachings. It was only a matter of identifying the appropriate article and the most effective trigger.

I just had to find a way to make sure that none of the one thousand delegates at the annual summit of religious leaders left the General Assembly building of the *United Nations* alive.

Strictly speaking this would not be mass suicide, more of a mass slaughter. But philosophically, laying down your life for a cause could be viewed by someone with the opposing cause as suicide. I was pleased with that thinking and so was the Order.

It had taken no more than a month of preparation. I had decided to induct just three delegates as the main players and eight others were primed to lock and guard the auditorium's four exits. My speech was designed to incite very deep hatreds, but we assumed there would be some partially enlightened people there who would be immune. However, we calculated that the percentage would be low and they would be consumed in the carnage.

The three main characters were an archdeacon, a mullah and a Jew. They had the most to lose. Not in terms of numbers following their doctrines but in terms of World power.

The world population is roughly seven billion people. Christianity has two and a half billion followers and Islam has a billion. That is half the world's population in just two religions. The Jews are amazing; they have just fourteen million faithful, a comparatively tiny amount, less than one percent of the planet's population, but their world influence is astounding, very far reaching. Marvellous marketing and brand recognition. I was betting on the rabbi cracking first.

GERRARD G. GERRARD

19

W A R S

War, always an evil?

Sometimes war can be the lesser of two evils but every war, however justified, reduces human good and civilisation, often destroying in seconds what centuries built. Is that a bad thing?

Religious war can never be justified on purely moral grounds. None of the major faiths is bloodless; history reeks with the gore of their wars and persecutions, made all the more fabulous for being in essence as simple as this:

Cuntianity kills Wanklam because Wanklam does not agree with Cuntianity's imaginary friend.

Some believe that people should be left to believe what they like, so long as they harm no one else. But who knows where that might lead? Chaos theory talks of a butterfly flapping its wings in Tewkesbury causing a hurricane in Florida. Who is to say that someone thinking about how nice it would be if everyone thought the same doesn't cause someone else to give it a go and try to make everyone think the same? It has happened already: Hitler, Stalin, Mao and the advertising industry.

From a worldly point of view religious beliefs are at worst absurd and at best dangerous. The amount of freedom they are given in the public domain is astonishing. They really capture the human imagination and for this they must be admired.

Believed-in fairies should be kept at home as an entirely private matter and fanatics should be encouraged not to take themselves so seriously. But if these fairies can cause passion, imagination and the willingness to die then I say they should be studied and encouraged. Arthur Conan Doyle still believed in the Cottingley Fairies despite having Sherlock Holmes whispering in his ear, 'It's a photo hoax, you bell-end.'

When irritated by those who differ, the teachings advise turning the other cheek and not throwing bombs. Such violent reactions show little confidence in their beliefs. So what makes them go against the core teachings?

'People should be left to believe what they like, so long as they harm no one else. This is why they all had to die, Mister Mann.' That voice again.

I, as usual, sat perfectly still. I could feel him smile.

'That smile tells me you understand. It was glorious, I wish you could have seen it, such perfection. One thousand people purified. The rhythm and flow was exquisite. The bulging anomaly was erased; the sense of peace after the show was terrifying.'

I had taken to the stage and begun my talk. An array of weaponry was displayed on the floor in front of the stage within easy reach of the delegates.

'He has made his weapons his gods. When his weapons win, he himself is defeated.' The microphone had been set up for optimal hypnotic effect; I spoke into it with low measured resonance. The doors were locked and the guards had taken up their positions.

'The illusion of human progress is beautifully illustrated by the difference between the spear and the guided missile.'

I gestured from the far right to the far left of the spread of weaponry, from spear through to guided missile.

'Humans have grown cleverer but not wiser. It is a disgraceful reflection on our moral health that guns are neither rarer than gold, nor harder to find than peace in the present murder-infested misery of the world. If any of you are looking for the usual hope message, the usual placating 'together we can overcome this' speech then you will be disappointed.'

No one heard the murmurs of discord over the self-feeding resonant hum of the trance-inducing public address system; this focussed the attention more on the speaker and stilled any doubts about what was being said.

'I have nothing to offer but despair. No solution, no guidance, no comfort. The murderous grip of humanity's various ancient belief-systems is unavoidably here now, sprouting its bitter fruit. Innocents cannot defend against the frenzy of fanatics, and against technological might. Intolerance, bigotry, zealotry and hatred brutally divides humankind against itself.'

I took the *Kevlar* flame and impact-resistant mask from the lectern and placed it over my head.

'I wear this purple mask as a symbol of my allegiance to no race, as a symbol of allegiance to my own one true faith.'

I took the dark cloak (augmented with ceramic, titanium and polyethylene) from the stand to my left.

'I wear this cloak as a symbol of my allegiance to no class or strata of society, as a symbol of my allegiance to myself. I call upon the right of Noah, the inventor of wine. God sent a great flood to destroy man as he had become wicked. Noah was righteous and chosen by God to save man. Noah has many names; Naunet, Manu, Nuwa, Ziusudra, Toptlipetlocali. But he has only one religion.'

I descended from the stage and into the audience. I approached the primed rabbi. 'In Hebrew 'Noach', the tenth and last of the antediluvian patriarchs.' I touched his brow.

He triggered.

I approached the mullah. 'In Arabic 'Nuh', a mighty prophet of God.' I stroked his temple. He sighed.

I approached the archdeacon. 'In Christianity the son of Lamech, and the first true church builder.' I traced a line from cheekbone to cheekbone. He gasped.

The rabbi was first, lunging for the flame-thrower, then the priest favouring the *Uzi 9mm* and then, somewhat reluctantly, the Mullah chose the Hunga Munga.

20

I N F E R N O

The Angel of Death walked, purple-masked and black-cloaked, through the mayhem, encouraging pockets of stillness, persuading the frightened to get involved. The rabbi's action with the flame-thrower had turned the auditorium into a furnace. The walls burned; the sprinkler systems disabled and no alarms sounded. The other religious leaders were embracing the tradition of violence, seizing weapons and employing them to dispatch their enemies.

The first to die were the atheists, invited as a courtesy to express their secular world-view. This pleased me. I disliked atheists more than the religious. Their simplistic smug arguments and sneering attitudes to things they did not understand. Using the outmoded theory of evolution to justify their cause, not realising that they are born into limitation or that the mind is an imperfect tool that can only be used to fathom rudimentary concepts. Probability and the scientific method, they deserved to die more than most.

Wrong, wrong, wrong.

Wipe them out let them start again.

I thought it might have been the Hindus who got it first, since Hinduism is the oldest extant religion and all other religions have evolved from it. That really upsets the other religions and they all vigorously deny their origins. But the Hindus came in a modest third.

The Buddhists were second. Easy target. Not putting up much of a fight, peaceable ways, and balance. Shame, but it is still a religion, a man-made corruption of the truth, it therefore deserves to die.

I passed amongst the faithful; the violence erupted in my wake, a gliding wave of destruction sweeping the room. The effect was again more than I had anticipated; all the delegates were embracing my doctrine. The guards at the exits weren't needed. This flock wasn't leaving.

I chose my spot and waited. Rictus grin and shrouded frame, observing the anger. Bodies burnt, shot, hacked, split. Heads crushed, splintered, wrought, severed. Limbs torn, sheared, minced, cleaved. Minds freed.

Finally it stopped. One man was standing. The survival of the fittest was not an atheist. His allegiance could not be fathomed by the torn, stained raiment he wore. It did not matter he was no longer human.

I gestured, the animal triggered, the animal fell.

PART
TWO

21

S L E E P

And so you judge me, you are me, I am you.

Everyone likes sleep but fears death, but the only difference is the length of time. You go to sleep and where does this world go? It is only a projection of your mind, of your thinking. Mind out, everything out. You wake up and you recreate this world again. We all do it, in agreement with each other; a skyscraper there, a swimming pool here, a road, a dog, a woman, a baby, a murdering psychotic. We are all to blame.

I needed a lie down after the last performance.

Most people like sleep but fear death. The only difference is the length of time.

I was twenty-five when I decided to sleep. I had done some things I wasn't proud of but I had really progressed in my spiritual path, got rid of a lot of baggage. And I had also persuaded two thousand one hundred and forty-two people to reconsider their lives, a good piece of community work in my opinion. I had helped the Order with their problem and I was no longer any use to them. They tried to kill me but I cannot die unless I choose. And I chose to live.

They sent the remaining Xaja after me as I knew they would. Shame they were no match. I freed a few more, they are with me now but the majority chose madness.

And now I wanted to sleep and grow. The best way to hide is to sleep. You go to sleep, deep dreamless sleep. And where does this world go? It disappears. And the struggles and the pain it inflicts are gone. If I slept they would not disturb me. I decided to sleep for thirteen years.

I sat in my room, my sanctuary, in my 1984 special edition *Parker Knoll Ambassador Deluxe* - in my opinion the finest piece of upholstered elegance money can buy. The simplicity of the manual recline, the choice of durable yet luxurious nylon cloth, the elegant robust lines and contours of a masterpiece.

I had read that fakirs in India would often go into a state of suspended animation, slow the body metabolism to barely a whisper and lie in that state undisturbed for tens and hundreds of years. They would emerge from their sleep not a day older, to them it seemed as if an evening had passed, but in reality years had. And so I slept dreamless sleep; reclined and gone from the physical world. My metabolism slowed to a ghost.

But it was not the complete dreamless sleep of the fakirs. I was tormented by the anger calling me back to the world. Injustice, I had things to do. That state beyond the body, beyond the mind, beyond space and time was within reach but the hate kept calling.

I slept and I grew, expanding into the universe like the unlimited being I am, infinite in knowledge and power and joy. But I realised I hated and so the joy was tainted with that hate, hate for everything in the world. All the fear, apathy, grief, anger and pride I felt was just a form of hate. And the hate called me back, nagged at me, asked me to look at it again, to relish in its delicious fire, cleansing the metal, making the world's impurities rise to the surface to be skimmed off. But traces still remained. It is so difficult to get anything really clean, wash three times with double distilled water, and dry with acetone... still a blemish. Microscopic but there, scrub, scrub, out, out, go away. Lance with torch, burn, destroy. Why won't it be clean? Why is it still marking, leaving a trace? No justice, no purity, just stains and hurt.

It was eventually time to wake up. Disturbed and tormented. I had grown, I had aged slightly, it was not a complete let go. My body showed faint signs of wasting. Lean, the fat reserves used. My hair longer, nails longer. My beautiful insect display case was still there to greet me, to remind me. And I woke reborn into the physical world. I had become without emotion.

I needed to come down. I needed to become human again. So I watched television hour after hour, for days, weeks. I walked around London and I watched. Willing the emotion back, I could feel it calling very softly, I had almost let go. I watched and walked for seven years before I had my first emotion.

It was *Forrest Gump*, the bit where Hanks says, 'He got a daddy named Forrest, too?' and Gump and his six year-old son watch television together holding hands. A tear formed at the side of my eye and slid down the gaunt alabaster. I leapt for joy and applauded my achievement. I laughed. I cried. I stared. I growled. I angered. Until.

Train.

It wasn't perfect.

I need the perfection.

I need the purity.

'Run, Forrest, Run. Mister Mann got a daddy named Mister Mann too.'

22

CRUELTY

It was the year 2008 and watching all that TV had taught me that the world had really moved on in my absence. Emotional pain is much worse than physical pain. Physical pain has an ending. The world had got a lot better at inflicting mental pain. Mister Li and his order had been busy and so had the dissenting factions. It was clear to me that TV had become little more than voyeuristic pornography. Reality shows everywhere. Even the supposed highbrow programmes were masturbating to the rhythm of condemnation. Hour after hour of so-called experts feeding the middle classes the diet of disapproval at these tawdry shows.

If they wanted pornography I'd give them pornography.

The atrocities had grown. War had increased. It seemed that my little display to the religious had only taught them to follow suit. The Twin Towers, a fantastic piece of psychological warfare. Simplicity. I learnt something there.

I sat in my *Parker Knoll* and plotted. I thought about my previous achievements. The train bothered me. It was all a bit contrived. It lacked simplicity. It annoyed me that it was so complicated. I sat and brooded, playing with my emotions, practising my scales like a musician. Apathy to Grief minor, leaping to Anger and back down to Fear major, resting for a beat on Lust. I noticed my hands began to spark. Tiny flashes of electricity passed from my finger tips as I riffed through the emotions.

That was new.

I held my hands to my head and thought Emotion. Sparks flew into my frontal lobe. I felt severe raging anger. The room that housed my *Parker Knoll* will never be the same. The walls cracked from my blows. Ceiling ruptured. All furniture, except for the *Ambassador* recliner and my insect cabinet, was obliterated. I thought Apathy - electric currents flowed from my fingers into my neocortex. I slumped. I came to three days later.

I thought Grief. Spark. He got a daddy named Forrest, too? And so on through the range, practising controlling until I was ready for my symphony.

23

T R A I N

I was going for purity, as nature intended. I boarded the train naked. No props, no preparation, just me. Heads turned. My torso lean, cut sinew moving gracefully. My hair long, past the shoulders. Despite being over forty now, no grey had appeared. Blonde flowing locks, slight curl. I moved down the carriage as the doors closed and locked, I introduced myself.

'I am Mister Mann and I am your conductor!'

My fingertips sparked in anticipation and I touched her temple. She rose, opened her handbag, removed the pen and stabbed the jugular of the man leering at her opposite. She stabbed and stabbed at his neck, screaming into his eyes, the undressing eyes that had raped her every morning for the last five years. He fell limp and she went to work on those eyes, now there would be no interference. I had unleashed something there. Incredible what people bottle up.

People stirred. A commotion at this time of the morning, surely not?

I moved deliberately, unhurried. There was all the time in the world. Time is an illusion.

I reached forward stroking his brow, sparking into the amygdala. Rage. Just the right amount. I needed a decoy, a focus for the have-a-go-hero, try to calm him down as I got to my diabolic work.

'Easy, mate! It's OK, he's only having a laugh, Rag Week or summin'. Here, mister, put your clothes back on. Nah, mate I'm not taking the… '

That's more like it. If you're going to try to stop

someone, move fast. No room for error. His tongue bitten from his head.

This was a lot more satisfying. Amazingly inventive, people. What was I thinking before? Suggestion, guidance, prop providing. No, just the suggestion will do.

Two people triggered and the pandemonium was building. People scarcely notice my buff, naked frame now. More pressing details to contend with. I struck a pose. Like an orchestral conductor. I pointed to the violins. Time for some exciting scaling. I lunged and touched a male and a female. My arms, outstretched cruciform. Sparks flew. Apathy. They no longer wanted to live and died immediately. God that felt good. What a rush. Double immediate suicide in zero point five seconds! A new personal best, ladies and gentlemen.

Some people were staring, they didn't fully appreciate the skill involved in that manoeuvre and I didn't have time to explain. I pounced, triggering all five in that small group. Who cares who won that fight, I was still rushing from the double suicide. It was as if there was a hive mentality operating, they sensed the next evolution and they were willing to die for it.

The carriage descended quickly into Hell. Not a single passenger untouched by my music. Time to trigger the next carriage before we arrived at Colchester and fresh meat arrived. Would they blindly join the train or sense something was wrong? This would be interesting. I toyed with using a Britney Spears type microphone to jam the station platform announcement system and issue commands, but that would've lacked the purity I was looking for. I wanted to be free of props and the tyranny of clothes. I sensed something would resolve and I would be granted my opus. I just needed to let go and let God.

I walked through the adjoining doors into the next carriage. The first to look: I took his head in my hands and got intimate. His sleepy eyes widened awake. I had his full attention. He was my special one.

'I am Mister Mann. You are special. So very special.' Blue line entered his skull. 'Do you understand how special, how noble in reason, how infinite in faculty! In form and moving how express and admirable! In action how like an angel, in apprehension how like a god! The beauty of the world. The paragon of animals! Do you see?'

Red sparks briefly burst. The special one smiled and saw.

'But I have of late lost all my mirth, this goodly frame; the earth seems to me a sterile promontory. And this most excellent canopy, the air, this brave overhanging firmament, this majestical roof fretted with golden fire, it appears to me like a foul pestilent congregation of vapours.'

The special one stopped smiling, the joy giver was unhappy. Blue cracks appeared.

'Man delights not me: no, nor woman either. Alas I cannot play the Dane. Will you play him for me?'

The special one rose and walked and disappeared into the third carriage.

People watched the performance. Someone clapped. She wouldn't applaud for long.

There was no reason to quote *Hamlet*; all the intricate commands were done with my fingers. I spoke Shakespeare for my own amusement. It seemed fitting.

Plagiarism is a noble tradition. It could be argued that there is no original thought. Newton himself said we stand on the shoulders of giants. He has been implicated in stealing his students' and contemporaries' ideas. In short, he was a nasty little thief. And Shakespeare was a nerd, the only one of a troupe of second rate actors who could read and write and so he gets all the credit. Shakespeare's plays are extremely variable in quality, indicating that they are from many sources. Shakespeare and his company had to compete with prostitution, cheap booze, cock fighting, circus and freak shows to earn a living. The amount of time they could indulge in decent prose was severely limited as the attention span of 15th Century man was short. The siren call of the mead and mammary in the tavern next door meant they had to quickly get to the anal raping of virgins: 'Take her away, use her at thy pleasure. Crack the glass of her virginity, and make the rest malleable.' (*Pericles*, *IV.vi.141-43*). Those boys knew how to engage the mind, to keep attention. All that cross-dressing, simulated sex with young boys, and references to old saggy breasts must have brought the house down. To think that Prince Charles used to regularly make speeches about Shakespeare's glorious contribution to our literary birthright, berating schools for 'destroying our heritage' by *not* pedalling the Bard's filth to young impressionable minds. Charlie later expressed a desire to be Camilla Parker Bowles' tampon. Who'd have thought? All the clues were there. And people are worried about the effect of video games.

So, plagiarise to make a living, many have made fortunes from literary theft. Just nick an idea from any short story by Phillip K Dick. Hollywood has been doing this for years and has made in excess of one billion American dollars. Poor old Dick didn't see a cent of it. He died shortly after *Blade Runner* was released, and the moguls capitalised on their 'relationship' by then releasing *Total Recall, Minority Report* and *Pay Check*, to name but a few. Or if film isn't your bag, how about books? Make off with a few ideas from this novel, sanitise them, make them palatable for the average human's sensibilities. Do a Gervais or a Pasquale, steal ideas from Stuart Lee and Michael Redfern. No one will care, except the original author, and in this case that's me and I don't give a damn. Knock yourself out. No one will know. Most ordinary people won't have read past the first page of this novel and those reading this far will be either too busy trying to get themselves out of a drug-induced coma or several steps ahead of you and on their second mediocre blockbuster novel. There is no such thing as original thought. Shakespeare stole from his more talented but lazy friends, who thieved from Ben Johnson who pilfered from Chaucer who invented a time machine and shagged J K Rowling. So it is all rubbish. J K writes derivative nonsense cleverly designed so vacuous parents can relate briefly with their immature stunted children. Read Tolkien and have a meaningful conversation. The original idea is the genius and people think that it needs improving upon. Like the hamburger, a marvellous creation but *McDonald's* comes along and turns it into something unrecognisable. The word 'hamburger', ironically, sums it all up: Beef doing all the leg work, pork taking the credit. And Harry Hill taking all the acclaim for that joke, not the bloke he overheard telling it in the pub.

Go on. Plagiarise. It makes sense. All the hard work has been done for you, and if it doesn't take off, nothing is lost.

People have gifts but it matters little what they do with them. My gift is freeing people, making them realise the futility of what they do. I could use my talents to make them feel better about themselves and so propagate the illusion and in the end the world dies to itself through a process of adsorption, billions of self-satisfied souls glorifying in the wonder of the individual. But I choose the difficult path because it is easy for me. I see the mess of the world the bitterness caused by people trying to be nice and not releasing their true nature, the pressure mounting through rule-following and conforming. I introduce another path, I point to the noble truth, the Ultimate Truth. You have to crack a few heads to make an omelette. And besides, if anything should happen to me at least I would be remembered. A man, one who makes everyone feel wonderful, makes strangers laugh, heals bitterness, brings happiness wherever he goes, gets killed and is immediately forgotten and the public attaches itself to another hero, that hive mentality again. That fragment of insecurity in me.

The woman clapped, and so that gesture of appreciation allowed her to be the next soul to be freed from pain. All entertainment is escape from pain. She wasn't happy with her own thoughts. My brief performance had taken her mind away from her feelings of inadequacy and she briefly felt better. Television, books, soap operas, plays, religion - all escapes from pain, all entertainment. The films you watch, even this book you read, the relationships you have, including the relationship you have with this book, are all escapes from pain.

Every time you feel happy your mind is at ease. Quieting the thoughts allows you to be and therefore to be happy, your natural inherent state. It is not the things that cause this quiet that provide happiness; it is the ability to be.

I took away her eyes.

'Do you see? Without those orbs of limitation you can be more yourself. You can see more clearly.'

She screamed. I took away the vocal chords.

'Do you understand? Without always trying to express yourself you can quiet the mind and be more yourself.'

She clawed at my face in panic. I paralysed her with a shock to the base of the spine.

'Be still and know that I am God. Do you comprehend? Now you are physically quiet your mind can be more still. And you should be able to feel more of yourself.'

My words were alarming her. Her ears started to bleed as I took away that limitation.

'You can hear me in your mind now. Can you see the Self? I am here to help, taking away your limitations so that you can be free. Do you see?'

She saw.

It's amazing how people will try to stop others helping others. All through that brief lesson the other passengers were trying to pull my naked form from her. I enjoyed the way they fell back dead - reinforcing the points I was making to the lady.

GERRARD G. GERRARD

24

T R A M P S

Before starting on the opus I observed an interesting new phenomenon since the big sleep. The homeless could enter my mind. Their thoughts direct and muddled. 'Spare some change mister, only a couple of quid for a bed tonight. One more punter and I'm done, I can rest.'

I could use this. The XAJA would come; I would make sure of that. They would be more powerful and I needed an army to cope with the nuisance.

I also had an idea to create the ultimate television pornography and the tramps could help. I needed their seed. That's why I didn't recruit the lady tramps. They were less powerful and direct in their thoughts. They were more consumed in the self. The outward projection to the world was faded and weak. They could rest.

I was sitting outside the *McDonald's* in Liverpool Street Station when I first became aware of the phenomenon. I was amusing myself by making the skanky grease pigeons shit on a young, gelled businessman. He was getting very irate, trying to keep the white slime from his burger, lashing at the pigeons, but had not yet moved inside to the safety of the McBuilding. Human tolerance for annoyance and pain is incredible. One of the reasons so many people work in London. No one would choose to work in the capital city. Greed invites them, sloth and inertia keep them chained, the slave consciousness.

The thought came, faint on the periphery:

laugh *look at that cunt* *laugh* *I wish I could do that* *have that ability* *laugh*

He'd noticed I was controlling the pigeons, he hadn't noticed he was projecting, not yet.

Loud, shock, make him awful.

YOU CAN HAVE THIS ABILITY *YOU ARE A CHOSEN ONE*

The tramp screamed and dropped to the floor, rolling. The pigeons scattered, the shit-covered barrow boy turned in the direction of the pain, annoyed that someone had a bigger problem.

I moved to the cowering wreck. Bent. Touched his temple. Caressed.

RISE *BE AFRAID OF NO ONE BUT ME* *CONTROL, MY SON* *CONTROL*

Colin Lomas stopped his writhing and stood up. With command, poise and menace, he saw the Truth. I stood back and watched what my disciple would do with his new powers.

He stared at the suited, ridiculous, arrogant jizznessman.

'What the fuck are you looking at? Look away before I beat you again, tramp!' Previous history these two – this could be interesting.

Lomas raised his arms, palms to the sky. Head fell back, eyes rolled. An angry sound emerged from a crack in the nearby building. Low angry hum. Rising to a scream.

'What the fuck are you doing? You fucking weirdo! Stop now or I'll fucking take your face off! Freak!'

The businessman was panicking. The sound was unnerving, Colin's theatrics unsettling. He sensed retribution.

Colin's voice boomed. 'Do? What am I going to do? Businessman I am going to turn you into a Buzznessman.' A dark cloud exploded from the crack in the building. Colin had found a nest.

'Vesper Vulgaris meet Homo Vulgaris!'

Lomas knew his insects, a man after my own heart.

The wasps swarmed the Buzznessman. They stung with fury. The man flayed, span, twirled, rolled and swelled. His gaudy metal watch glinted in the afternoon sun, winking faster and faster, a disco glitter ball to his death dance. His movement slowed, the wasps retired.

Colin smiled. 'Got any spare change, Buzznessman? What's that? You haven't finished living yet? Oh very funny, very witty, very droll!'

Colin kicked the swollen mess, a gentle tap with the tip of his tatty boot. 'Not finished living? I think you have.'

25

T R A I N

She saw. She let go. Her body died to this world. People stopped trying to help her and fear gripped the carriage. Some stayed in their seats; some were still reading the *Daily Mail* as if that paper would tell them how to leave this hell. Some ran to the next carriage. We would be at Colchester soon and those afraid ones would try to get off. Things were getting out of control. Chaotic. I wanted control. Why did I always want control? The want of anything indicates lack. If you want something it means you don't have it. It is wrong to want control but right to have control. I have control.

I had seen Lomas do it on several occasions with the insects. He would enter the hive mind and control them from king position. I had always feared the hive, the ability I sensed to be one, be one with the human hive, and possibly everything. It was always me, me, mew, mew, mewl, mewl, mewling, mewling idiot. Contempt for myself held me back.

All the passengers saw the train. But not one individual would see it exactly the same as another. As Albert Einstein said, 'Reality is an illusion, albeit a very persistent one.'

Reality is perception. The passengers all had their own perception of events. Each individual making up his own picture, layer upon layer of slightly different realities. Space and time does not exist. These pictures all exist at one point. To enter that point was the key. You can talk about String Theory, Causal Dynamical Triangulations, Quantum Einstein Gravity, Quantum Graphity or Internal Relativity if you must. But these just complicate the Truth. These models change and shift, twist and beguile. Truth never changes; anything that changes is a lie. These passengers were living their lies. The lies originated from a point, originated from the point of Truth. The trick was to enter that point and control, make up a lie for everyone and set them free.

It scared me to attempt it. I would lose my self, not just my carcass. This was The Ultimate Fear of Dying, fear of complete obliteration not just a beating of the body, this was *spirit*. Potential complete consumption, no coming back if I couldn't control it. It was good to be afraid of something again. Confront your fears. Grow. I was getting better, becoming more giving; more in touch with my emotional intelligence and the emotional and spiritual needs of others. I had freed many souls, nine thousand, nine hundred and ninety-nine so far. Nothing compared to Stalin, Hitler or Mao Zedong.

Stalin is widely believed to hold the record for democide with forty-three million people killed during his time in power from 1929-1953; this is double the amount that Hitler managed to bump off. But, on an annualised basis this only equates to one point four eight million for every year in power. In the Tyrant Top Ten the Number 1 spot goes to a woman, the Empress Dowager Cixi, with two point four million dissenters per year. She only managed to kill twelve million in total but had a very short reign of just five years. What a Mother Puss Bucket Bitch. The Number 1 spot should actually go to Mao Zedong who managed to kill seventy-seven million during his time in power as head of the People's Republic of China. But westerners don't like to criticise the Chinese for fear of dying, and so they get away with it.

All these mass murderers were despotic, totalitarian, dictators with no concern for others. I am not like them, I help people deliberately. They were helping people without knowing. My nine thousand, nine hundred and ninety-nine souls are but a vinegar stroke compared to their horse cum efforts. But who knows what I might create in the future or, indeed, what someone else might create? The histories of Barack Obama, Gordon Brown and Angela Merkel have yet to be written.

Perhaps I should just use the Emotion Pulse to control those passengers that are running. Elegance, Mister Mann, elegance. The EP is barbaric in comparison, good but not compared to the simple beauty of entering the Point. *Eminem* vs. *Pink Floyd*. Jack Black vs. Gerard Hoffnung. Phillip K. Dick vs. Frank Herbert.

    William Shakespeare vs. Gerrard G. Gerrard.

26

E M O T I O N   P U L S E

I approached the private members' club. My thirst raged. The guards on the door, keeping out the plebs, moved aside. They knew not to ask.

I descended the stairs to the main room. Large, cluttered with the gaudy trappings of the Mayfair set. Gold embossed deep pile elegance to keep everyone safe. They knew they'd be secure, not badgered by the riffraff, by the common man. But I am everyman and can do what I please.

The bartenders were busy tailoring cocktails to the exquisite palates of their rich clientele, radar scanning the room for the tips, the money. The *maître d'* making sure everyone felt special, reserving the deepest bows for those who'd really appreciate them. The wallet vampires perched. The enhanced women, disguised by make-up and plastic surgery, surveyed the room, looking for the Alpha Male, the biggest killer, the Darwinian prize. I was standing in the centre of the bar area.

The menu was expensive and ridiculous. Faux world cuisine with a French twist. Always the words fusion to disguise the reality of the failed alcoholic chef churning overpriced confections.

I moved around the area breathing in the soul. I sensed disaster. I sensed a cleansing. I sensed the anger rising. All that was wrong with the world was summed up here. The rich getting richer while the poor got poorer, and for what? For a few to play a pointless game. I could hear the repeated slogans:

'He who dies with the most toys wins.'

'Kill or be killed.'

'So, what first attracted you to the millionaire Paul Daniels?'

Everywhere blonde supermodels, fuzzy-faced Arab types, greasy city buffs living the dream. Time to turn that dream to a nightmare. Time for a lesson.

Walk away, Mister Mann, leave it, they ain't worth it. Live and let live. NO.

Leave, please leave, forgive them, for they not know what they do. YES.

They are children obsessed with their own importance; they need to grow up and learn the lesson. No.

I am going, I just need to walk up those stairs and disappear into the night and everything will be all right. Yes.

And then she approached. Enhanced Uber-Woman, fresh from the exquisite cocaine snorting facilities out the back, eyes buzzing, plumped lips smacking. Radar fully operating, she had found the Alpha Male of her dreams. She made her opening gambit, leaned in to me, sniffed deeply at my chest, expert hands caressing my shoulders.

'I smell spunk, I love spunk. I want your spunk.'

Her intonation was perfect. No doubt this chat-up line had worked on every high powered male she had ever ensnared.

I replied loudly. 'How fucking dare you! Who do you think you are? You're not fit to receive my shit up your rancid hole, what right do you have to my seed?'

The room went quiet.

She froze.

My anger rose.

'How can anyone get precious about bodily fluids? Aircrafts recycle flatus that people breathe in for the entire journey, pressure changes causing bodies to pass wind, three hundred squeezed bags crammed into a fuselage.

'There is excrement all around you. On the peanuts here, on that surface, on your hands and face, on computer keyboards. Shit is everywhere, and it's not just your own. Public transport seats are covered with semen, urine and faeces. We are surrounded by bodily fluids, how can anyone get so precious about them?

'How dare you get precious about *my* semen?'

I had never experienced such anger before. What a disgusting slut - crude, vain, presumptuous. My anger peaked, I grabbed her ears.

'When does an immature girl who smells of piss and fish change into a voluptuous woman who's good enough to eat? Never! Look really hard and you'll see it's just an illusion: supermodels, prostitutes, tarts like you, every woman still smells of piss and fish. Wake up!'

And then it happened.

The pulse of rage shook the room. A visible blue energy radiated from my centre and engulfed the room. Everyone in that building was stunned and stood motionless.

Be not the doer, Mister Mann. Be the observer.

Interesting.

I could see by the small frightened movements of her eyes that she was not completely paralysed. I let go of the object of my hate. I looked at the others, they were similarly affected; they could witness me but not move. I went to work.

Looking back now, it was the exotic food menu and the strumpet's coke addiction that inspired me. I noticed that Chinese food was poorly represented on the menu and decided to address the balance. I recalled the 1978 mondo film *Faces of Death*. A few minutes preparation and she was ready for her lesson.

'What made you approach me?' I allowed her to speak.

'I'm sorry, sir, the drug made me bold, I'm sorry,' she sobbed.

The others stared at her, no one offering to help. No one speaking for her. The top half of her head was protruding from the middle of a table, the sides of her face cut by the wooden shards from the hole punched hastily through.

'You were oblivious to the danger. You didn't see the warning signs. You were numbed by the drug. I understand. Don't worry, I understand. It was a choice you made. Take responsibility for the choice. Do not blame the drug. You are now here, in this table, part of this table. Learning your lesson.'

She wanted to speak, I did not allow it.

'And your friends, the alpha males that previously wanted you so badly, more than all the other greed vampires, are now silent, not defending your honour. How sad, not one speaking out in protest, even their eyes are silent. Watching but silent.'

Her eyes darted, the top of her skull had been removed with a knife. Her body beneath the table was motionless.

'Do you like television advertisements from the 1970s? Can you remember that far back? Coke is also a soft drink. A drink that has beaten off all competition to dominate the world.

Her exposed brain glistened in the light of a flickering candle. Moist fluids straining to keep the organ alive.

'You have enhanced your body beyond your genetic makeup. Breasts, lips, cheeks, forehead, buttocks, legs, undoubtedly your vagina and anus have had treatment too. I applaud you, that shows commitment to the illusion of life. There's nothing I like more than someone who shows an intention. Your intention to become what you became is a marvel.'

A rivulet of blood escaped a cheek wound, joining the movement of eyes, all else remaining still.

'And you use a drug to enhance your brain. Interesting, but misguided. Have you seen what *Coke* does to teeth? Have you seen what *coke* does to a brain?'

I poured a generous scoop of the powder directly onto her exposed brain; aiming for the cerebral cortex, the controller of higher functions. It fizzed and popped on contact with the protein-rich protective fluid.

'It's frothy, man!'

'*Cresta*,' she sighed. A childhood memory triggered.

'LIPIDSMACKIN'
BURSTWENCHIN'
GOODBUZZING'
FOOLTALKIN'
HIGHWALKIN'
FASTLIVIN'
NEVERGIVIN'
FOOLFIZZIN'
MONKEY WHORE!'

'*Pepsi.*' The word dropped vaguely from her mouth. Her eyes watered and blinked out. She had learnt the limitation of enhancement. I tipped the rest of the cocaine onto the dying organ. 'I'd like to teach the world to sing in perfect harmony. Who's next?'

The others just stared, emotion pouring from their eyes.

There was only one other that I felt compelled to teach. I had listened to his endless prattle before the interruption from the Monkey Whore. He had been holding court, telling stupid stories about his reckless youth, about when he was daring and free, silly tales of naked drinking and being chased by the police, fantasies of taking risks with crowds of niggers, about fighting for people's honour. Meaningless drivel designed to impress and shock. He'd had the chance to go into space on a *NASA* scientific mission but that was put back because of the *Challenger* exploding, and so he'd sought his fortune in the City. He'd been suggestive to the ladies, pretending he understood their needs, commenting on breast size and the importance of a decent dress, he had been giving the women present alpha status hoping they would feel comfortable and join him in expressing his Nazi sentiments. Meaningless conspicuous consumption, a parody, a young man in danger of turning into the fat cunt in the corner surrounded by the Eastern European wallet vampires. I sensed, as I did with everyone I had ever met, that he meant well, but had missed the point. He annoyed me more than the whore and for that I thanked him in my own way.

'NAME?' I allowed him to speak.

'Andrew Gerrard Wilkins.'

'DIE!'

He is with me now. They all are.

27

T R A I N

The Emotion Pulse was not to be used, too crude. Too much drama, too time consuming, although time is an illusion. I cared in those days, I really wanted to save people, I really wanted to improve the world. I wanted to change it. Now I could not care less. I was so arrogant, not realising that the world is perfect, as it should be. I could not see the perfection where the seeming imperfection seems to be. Silly Mister Mann. Let go and let God, Mister Mann. No. Control and be sure. Control, Mister Mann. Yes.

Sometimes I think I'm going insane, but I know too much for that to happen. I couldn't go insane even if I tried. Insanity comes from deep terrible apathy, I am nowhere near apathy. If I wanted, I could go out of my mind; I don't have to think if I don't want to. I could move into knowingness, and act, do things that just come to me on the spur of the moment. Like a hunch or intuition. Operating in knowingness without thinking, I don't have to think. That is not insanity, that is the opposite end of the scale. Let go and let God.

I moved through the carriage and let the sparks fly. Touching, spinning, kneeling, caressing, letting myself become part of them. They became part of me, we danced together. I did not think, and so have complete accurate recollection of the ingenuity of the people on board the train that day.

Colchester arrived, the passengers stilled, people boarded the train unsuspecting, others sensed the danger and hesitated - their loss, the cowards. The doors closed, the carnage continued. And so on through the carriages I moved, persuading people to join me.

I stayed on the train at Stratford, the time before I had got off, not willing to die in the crash. I didn't care if the train was to be completely consumed, didn't care if there would be survivors. I knew there would be just one.

I felt the driver's mind. He agreed.

We pulled gently into Liverpool Street Station. The doors to the first carriage opened. I stepped out in my new suit of blood and flesh. The platform was eerily empty and quiet.

The Dane emerged from the driver's cabin in a trance. My Hamlet had done his work. I touched his brow. He thanked me and dropped to the floor, released from his torment.

My thoughts turned to the monkey woman and the private members' club. How similar that scenario, to this one on the train; humans struggling with the slave consciousness, testosterone fuelling atrocities and people prostituting themselves to make ends meet.

Alas poor Yorick, I knew him, Horatio.

Alas it's all bollocks, I knew the whore ratio.

28

P O R N O G R A P H Y

The train was a reminder, a wakeup call. The XAJA would come, but to make sure I needed to create something bigger than the train, something that couldn't be covered up by the familiar excuses of leaves on the line, overrunning rail works at Bethnal Green or failed points at Stratford. I needed something that would be very public.

My army of tramps had grown fast. Lomas was recruiting some strong soldiers too. We taught them the secret to making money, so they could be strong and anchored in the world. Supply is infinite, there is no need to compete, just take what you need.

As a payment for these teachings I demanded a sperm donation every day. They would have to masturbate into test tubes and deposit these at the collection point. I had considered robbing a sperm bank, but the amount and quality of spermatozoa was not sufficient. It had to be homeless humus.

My army had grown to three hundred members. My Spunk Spartans. I needed three hundred litres from the members' members. The average single serving of ejaculate is somewhere in the region of six millilitres. So that was one hundred and sixty-six pops each. I was ready in six months.

Using my not inconsiderable charms I had persuaded a greedy executive at a grasping but popular television studio to give me my own chat show.

I was due to go live on air the day after the train atrocity. This was to be the next *Big Brother*, the next *Jerry Springer Show*, the next mould-shattering TV concept. The premise was to get intelligent, successful and articulate people to air their dirty washing. I was the host and the audience was composed of all the bastions of the light entertainment industry. The idea was to prove to the masses that everyone is the same; that the intelligentsia are no different from the trailer trash paraded on day time television.

I had proved, over six months in test programmes, that I had the ability to unearth the very deeply embarrassing secrets these seemingly controlled and respectable people held dear. I had demonstrated time and again that I could reveal startling histories. The people questioned were under the impression that they would be interviewed on their specialist subjects. Essentially 'The Mister Mann Probe' was Melvyn Bragg's The South Bank Show brought up to date to satisfy the modern appetite for emotional pornography.

They had bitten hard and thought I was a genius, their ticket to immortality. They were right of course but not in the way they had hoped.

My first guest was fifty-seven year-old Greta Amarillo, the well-respected water colour painter and member of the Royal Academy of Arts. She had been enjoying a recent renaissance as people tired of the Modern Art movement and the Turner Prize could no longer provoke shock due to programs such as the one I was hosting. This woman had talent, an ability to capture ordinary day-to-day scenes and infuse them with a sense of life, meaning and movement. Her work was excellent. A typical painting would involve a picnic, or a table set for a meal; food and family life were her focuses. She was posh, slightly pretentious and proud. Perfect. I talked around the subject of her paintings, highlighting her skill, appreciating her style, noting that food played a vital role.

'I notice that the humble anchovy always appears at every meal scene.' I produced a series of ten recent paintings and pointed out the tiny detail. Using the voice. 'Here. Here. Here, here, here. Here, here, here, here, and *here*! Why is that?'

'I like to smear anchovies into my vagina.'

A gasp from the audience, but her admission shocked her the most.

'And why is that?' The voice again.

'The smell and the texture, the tiny bones, lightly cutting, the abrasive salt stinging, it just does it for me.'

'OK, so it's fair to say that this pleasure spills over into your work and is partly responsible for the marvellous voracity, movement and honesty of your paintings.'

'I don't care, love, I just can't get enough of the fishy deliciousness.'

Stifled laughter from the audience.

I released her. She caught herself. Embarrassment, redness flushed, voice stammer, incomprehension as to what secret she had just admitted. She got up to leave, fell back, got up again and ran crying into the arms of the dutiful husband who waited for her in the wings.

That got their attention.

Hush fell on the audience. I waited a beat.

'Greta Amarillo, ladies and gentlemen. Beautiful paintings and beautiful honesty.'

Applause.

My next guest was thirty-five year-old Gavin Victoria, the contemporary dance choreography maestro. As homosexual as a fist full of peacock feathers. He flounced, sashayed onto the set, placed himself on the couch with pouting precision. A caricature, he made pink look like a very light red. He applauded the bravery of Greta and wished that there was more honesty like that in this world.

There would be.

The audience joined in with his dramatic and frantic clapping. We talked about his work, showing VT of his latest project *The Dance of the Testicle,* and I fed his ego and inflated his pride. He was exceptional, a talent for seeing movement, for recognising and pairing forms. We talked his subject. I offered a speculation.

'Gavin, the reason that your work is so well-respected and received is, maybe, because it comes from a *very male* point of view.'

'Well, I know men, if you know what I mean?' Gaudy wink. Audience laughter.

'Yes, and you also know women. You have one of the most exquisite understandings of pairings I have ever seen. The meaning of Yin and Yang is clearly demonstrated in your work. I'm guessing you are not homosexual.'

The audience laughed at the ridiculousness of the suggestion. Gavin was silent, contemplating his reaction. I had not used the Voice yet. The audience fell silent. 'You were saying earlier about honesty, Gavin?' No Voice.

'I don't know anymore. I love dance more than anything. *Billy Elliot* is a lie. The whole industry is run by queens. I slept my way to the top. I prostituted myself for the love of my art. I pretend to be gay to get the funding, but my work is honest. You develop a lie and become that lie; it's easier than telling the truth. It's easier than going back. Sex with men disgusts me but I do it for my love. At least, it used to disgust me, I'm not so sure now. It has become more of a bodily function, a necessary one, to pursue my love. There comes a point when you don't know if a thing is good or bad, live or dead, it just is. Do you know what I mean?'

'I know.'

Gavin left, head low but with rising applause from the audience.

'Ladies and gentlemen, Gavin Victoria, or should I say Gavin Victor?' Corny drum roll and laughter from audience.

My final guest was sixty-four year-old particle physicist, Professor Wilhelm Shutner.

'So, shall we talk about neutron scattering at the surfaces of colloids or cut straight to the chase?'

'I don't know what you mean.'

'Yes you do.'

The professor considered his options and was about to leave when…

'Your Matey is a bottle of FUN!' Full Voice.

'You put me in the bath!' The professor joined in.

'And why is it fun?'

'I love to go to Ibiza for foam rave parties. My wife thinks I'm at scientific conferences!'

Laughter from the audience. What a delightful show it had been so far, so much honesty. And a lovely light-hearted, essentially harmless admission to close on.

I waited for the laughter to subside and started on the closing monologue.

'And after all, what's wrong with all these quirks? As long as there is mutuality, consent, I see no harm. Granted, the anchovies haven't much say in the matter but I'd much rather be smeared on a vagina than be baked on a pizza (corny drum roll and laughter). And I know the professor has been economic with the truth about the foam raves but perhaps now his wife will throw aside her inhibitions and join the doc and have some fun. There is nothing wrong with foam rave parties; the sensation of the foam and the egalitarian way everyone looks the same can bring a strong sense of community.

'It does of course depend what the foam is made from. Soap is fun, but if it was tramp jizz it would in fact look, smell and taste disgusting and create an atmosphere similar… to… THIS… '

The cameras turned one hundred and eighty degrees onto the audience. The one hundred litre pressurised cans beneath the three cameras burst into action and sprayed the audience with grey foamy tramp spunk. Wide-eyed and open-mouthed, the peddlers of emotional pornography took their punishment. I had considered the Noel Edmunds gunge tank approach on just two members of the audience, the worst offending duo, for their nasty insidious Saturday night efforts: 'Let us take the piss out of your shitty little life and we'll give you a holiday'. But the two little perverts would actually have enjoyed the attention and three hundred litres of undiluted vagabond juice sliming over their insipid bodies.

The one hundred and fifty members were all guilty, and were all busy trying to figure out which of their showbiz 'friends' had set this one up, simultaneously attempting to put on a smiley show face and suppress outrage at their agents for not thinking of this first. Slowly, the smell of the foam started to take hold. Eyes started to sting and the realisation that this was indeed spunk took hold.

I considered killing them all, but these people were not in the body, they were only concerned with ego, approval and control. No, I wouldn't kill them. The psychological impact of this event would last years. The deaths of their careers would be pain enough.

The central camera turned to me.

'Ladies and gentlemen, you are probably wondering

why you are seeing these images and why the ten minute broadcast delay has failed to kick in. Well, Bob in Control is under *my* control. These people covered in tramp sperm are the devils and I am your Messiah. I am not a cuddly Messiah like Jesus, Buddha or the other one. I'm a Messiah that doesn't give a fuck about you. So carry on grabbing my attention, annoying me and I'll pay you a visit. I've been Mister Mann, you've been an audience. Goodnight!'

The camera turned to the grey-slimed, tramp foam bukkaked, rioting crowd. The credits rolled.

Ken Morse, as always, was on rostrum.

GERRARD G. GERRARD

29

T H E R M O S

God is not a creator, only man is. In the ultimate there can be no creation, as everything is perfect and needs no addition. The only creator is man and he created the heavens and earth. The earth is Hell.

I sat in my usual seat, sandwiches on the seat to my left, thermos flask in my lap. I haven't had food or drink for years now, since before the sleep. But I liked to know they were there just in case I got peckish. It was a lovely spot just to the right of Gate 10, over the way from Gate 20, past the main shops, away from the bustle, but not so much that the ebb and flow of human traffic stagnated. A vending machine to my right occasionally brought me out of my reverie with the clatter of falling metal. A half-caste boy was kneeling at the window looking at my view; control tower in the distance, runways in front, jumbos being towed into position. Heathrow was a fabulous airport. Every flying nation represented there.

It was the day after the television show and I wondered if the boy had been allowed to watch it and if he had, whether he'd enjoyed it. His turquoise *Velcro* fastened *Nike* trainers suggested he had; his bored expression as he looked away from another airplane taking off and gazed nonchalantly at me suggested he hadn't. Why do parents think kids like watching planes take off? Because it is exciting? No, because it looks to the inexperienced eye as if there's a good chance of a crash. But after seeing four or five successfully make it into the air this wise child was realising that planes in general don't crash. However, this was his lucky day.

GERRARD G. GERRARD

30

C H I L D R E N

And so you judge me.
You are me.
I am you.
Prepare to change.

I like children and this boy pleased me. Children are bastards, like all people, but they have only a few of the control mechanisms that have been forced on adults initially by school and later by the slavery most call a career. The young have not yet learnt to be completely imbecilic. Children are less brainwashed, more creative, more themselves. Most children are in fact traumatised by the birth experience and for the first fifteen years of their lives are almost drunk, barely awake and all they have to guide them are neurotic parents who are, in turn, paralysed by fear, controlled by the state, religion, society or disapproving glares from strangers. Babies emerge from the womb screaming in pain, hunger gnawing, forced to breathe air instead of the natural amniotic fluid. Unable to fend for themselves and told what to do. The only way they can gain approval is by emulating their parents, the only way they can gain control is by screaming and then they are punished if they protest too much. All this in the vain effort to gain security.

And so the process evolves; the blind leading the blind *ad infinitum*, descending spiral into disaster.

'The children now love luxury; they have bad manners, contempt for authority; they show disrespect for elders and love chatter in place of exercise. Children are now tyrants, not the servants of their households. They no longer rise when elders enter the room. They contradict their parents, chatter before company, gobble up dainties at the table, cross their legs, and tyrannise their teachers.' This was said by Socrates two thousand, four hundred years ago. I wonder what he'd make of the utter shits that have evolved today.

I thought about reproducing, but finding a suitable mate was tricky with so many freaks and weirdoes about.

I had a girlfriend once; a quadriplegic, no arms or legs, just a body and a head, beautiful face, sweet innocent mind. I could have loved her. Bob was her name, well it was actually Monica, but we went swimming once and the sobriquet stuck. She complained when I disappeared for three months on one of my walks. She complained I never told her I was going, I never wrote, I never telephoned. When I got back she was angry and she had shacked up with someone else, thinking I was dead. Needy bitch.

I had always considered the happiest marriage as one in which each partner lives only for the other's happiness. I used to long for a little woman to raise my children, make a home, I'd share the chores in a fair but manly way.

But I had been looking at marriages. Tricky. Best left alone. I decided to pursue my goal alone. I decided to go for freedom.

The thing that links people is the pursuit of happiness, it's the one thing that everyone has in common, they're all striving for that bit of joy. Constant joy without pain, is that possible?

Yes it is.

Shall I tell you how? No, I shan't. Why? Because I despise you.

Do I have constant happiness without sorrow? No, I don't. Why? Oh, I know how to achieve it, but I won't let myself, I won't let myself remember. Why? Because I despise myself more than I despise you.

And that, in a nutshell, is the only reason people get married. They despise themselves; meet someone who makes them feel good, but because of past relationships they know deep down that it won't last. So why bother? Because there is the more pressing subconscious lure of the new love, the potential to despise someone more than themselves and thereby feel better.

But, enough of sentimentality, I had a plane to crash.

GERRARD G. GERRARD

31

C R A S H

The Hassidic Jew rocks himself and strokes his locks, muttering prayer. A businessman twitches and stares into his laptop computer. A lady lifts her belongings from the security tray, adorns herself with jewels. Strangers walk by, seemingly talking to themselves, then their heads turn to reveal bluetooth ear devices. Everywhere people twitch, shuffle, and shift. Everyone is suffering from *Tourette's Syndrome* to some degree. There are no calm people. There are no people at peace in this place. No one glides. Everyone is stressed.

Tourettes - most suffer from reverse *Tourettes*; the inability to protest. What's to say that the touretto is not the lucky one, the normal one, but is unlucky because the rest of society has ganged up on him and made it socially unacceptable to protest without provocation. The rest of society has learnt to suppress this natural instinct to call a cunt a cunt, and thereby alienates the gifted touretto. If a touretto is left alone he is quiet. It is the observation of a touretto that causes the yelping and twitching.

The Mister Mann Touretto Uncertainty Principle: you can predict the frequency of a yelp or where he will explode, but not both.

Zen Tourettes: A touretto in a forest alone yelping, does he make any sound?

Enough of this musing, they all had *Tourettes* to some degree, all were stressed and it was time to take the cortisol levels up.

The boy sensed and looked my way.

JAT
SAS
BMI
BBA
GULF
DELTA
VIRGIN
UNITED
QANTAS
OLYMPIC
AIR INDIA
EMIRATES
SWISS AIR
AER LINGUS
SINGAPORE
AIR ASTANA
AIR ALGERIE
LUFTHANSA
JET AIRWAYS
STAR ALLIANCE
BRITISH AIRWAYS
ROYAL JORDANIAN
ETHIOPIAN AIRLINES
TURKMENISTAN AIRLINES
KLM ROYAL DUTCH AIRLINES

So much choice.

Qantas and *Aer Lingus* stood out: the first for brazen disregard for conventional spelling, the second for sounding like a sex act. I settled on *Virgin* for the hypocritical suggestion of purity.

Mister Mann has control.

The boy turns back to the view, ready for the show. I probe the plane for emotion; the nervousness of a takeoff, apprehension. The plane accelerates and hearts race.

Soothe:

Planes don't crash, we'll be OK.

Thrust pushing bodies into chairs, committed to flying. The subtle heavy-lightness as the wheels leave the ground, accentuated gravity pressure again. Wing wobble, beat miss, stabilise, incline and climbing. Incline too steep?

Mister Mann has control.

Straining engines, air sucked and pushed. Too steep, is something wrong? Wing dip, beat missed, slow turn, it is climbing but steep.

Mister Mann has control.

Plane slows, too slow. Engines squeal, wings flex and strain. Too steep.

Mister Mann has control.

The plane stalls and dips, flat-bellied plummet, slight spin-turn to ground.

Mister Mann has control.

The plane flat tanks into the fuel depot, exploding into freedom. Panic in tower, chief air traffic coordinator calm.

Mister Mann has control.

Six planes ordered to leave the ground now, danger too great. All planes under control. Meet in air in between tower and Mister Mann's position. Iron cluster intercourse ejaculates fire.

Mister Mann releases control.

The boy turns to Mister Mann.

'Wow! Did you see that, mister?'

'Yes.'

'That was much better than your show last night.'

'Yes.'

'What you going to do next, something horrible again?'

'Yes.'

'Can I have your autograph?'

'No, you cunt.'

Kids, eh?

32

V A G I N A

If you suppress a word you give it power. To me no word is disgusting. All are beautiful. Language is gorgeous.

Take the word 'cunt'. Why do so many people get upset at the use of that word, especially women and Americans? What's not to like about the word cunt? The object itself brings such joy, sensation and life. OK the word itself suggests a lack of hygiene, but if you lick and polish it enough it soon becomes fresh and tasty, so get involved.

Start using the word. Wrap your tongue round it, caress it, get rough with it, spit at it, use it, become its master, you will soon see the seeming unpleasant thing becomes a tame and good-natured beast. Through suppression, the word has ended up as one of those angry bellicose vaginas from the seventies: hairy, unkempt, brutal. With a bit of attention and use it can be an inviting modern hole of the 21st Century with neatly trimmed topiary. The trauma of birth is such that men spend a lifetime trying to get back up there, and women try to find any means to plug the hole, to stop more nastiness coming out. Some men think God is a woman's vagina; others think God is another man's arsehole. Would God choose to hang out in these places? You see how foolish this thinking is? Did Jesus talk to Mary's vagina or Barrabbas's backside when he pleaded to his dad on the cross? Ask him. I'll ask him now. The only difference between priests and madmen? The people they talk to.

No, Jesus says that he looked to the sky, but he also says that God is everywhere so it doesn't really matter where you direct the questions. And besides, he says he wasn't pleading he was proving, proving that you do not die, that it is impossible to die. And he really wishes the Christians would stop wearing crosses around their necks, coz it wasn't that easy to get crucified and it still gives him a peculiar feeling thinking about and being reminded of it. Are they taking the piss? Any emblem would be better than the cross; fish, loaves, symbol of infinity, anything. It's one of the reasons he hasn't come back, because two and a half billion people have missed the point and insist on wearing and erecting that instrument of torture in his name. What's that, Jesus? You'll come back if they replace the crucifix with the cunt, the life giver? OK, I'll see what I can do.

The reason sex is so popular and these objects, the penis and vagina, are given such status is that sex quiets the mind. People will do anything to get a few seconds of quiet from an orgasm. Quiet mind and happiness shines forth, the true nature emerges. Again, looking for happiness where it does not exist. Happiness is not in the external world, it is within. Where does the world really exist? In your mind, mind out - world out. It is very simple.

So, cunt is good. And that is why I called the cheeky kid who asked for my autograph at the airport a cunt. And that is why his mum got upset and that is why she tried to control me and that is why the kid is now an orphan. The power of cunt!

33

E D U C A T I O N

Education is learned ignorance. No one teaches how to be happy. What is taught is how to be a good slave. The basic subjects: Maths, Language, all designed to help society prosper. And so the majority commute vast distances to sit at desks and shuffle. Wishing their lives away for the four meagre weeks a year when they can be entertained and put out of their misery. Two weeks if they're American.

Most jobs could be done in less than two hours a day, if people thought about what they were doing and coordinated and cooperated with each other. Outrageous statement? Check and see.

What is the solution? Thinking and using discrimination to get yourself off of automatic. And bravery. It takes courage to leave the captor. *Stockholm Syndrome*. Walk away and let it happen. You will not die. You will become more yourself. You will become happier and lighter. Your friends will scorn, rally against you, bite, scratch and tear you back to the fold. That hive mentality again. Resist, become a sentient. What friends?

Education is just another form of separation, the elite schools around the world inviting you to join their alumni if you are an exceptional slave. The richest most successful people in the world are drop-outs and visionaries, they haven't been indoctrinated into the mill of B.Sc., M.Sc. and Ph.D. Bullshit, More Shit and Pile it High and Deep, as countless students have chanted in humour, all the while feeling there may be truth behind the joke.

It's only the lower class education centres that

produce the heroes that go on shooting sprees. Usually in an American town that nobody knows. The reason for this is that the grip of the educators is not strong enough and people have the opportunity to resist the indoctrination and to rise up against it and make a choice: serfdom or freedom. And these martyrs are kind enough to take a few other captives to freedom too.

A class massacre would never happen at Oxford, Cambridge, Harvard, *MIT*, *INSEAD*, Princeton or Reading. The educators are too strong and compelling to lose their grip on the incumbents.

Guess what?

Yep.

34

L I

I was watching the crashed planes and confusion. Alarms sounding, fire engines racing the runway, and people screaming; mindless as usual but with slightly more focus. The half-caste was staring at his mother. She was on the floor, by the window, dead. The boy tried to comprehend.

Mister Li appeared with nine Xaja. My exit was behind them, the security check by Gate 20. They formed a semi circle, Li in the middle, five Xaja to his right and four to his left, hemming me in, blocking my way out. I sensed a hive mind in operation. Mister Li spoke with deliberate tones, and powerful use of the Voice. He was using the power of the nine to enhance, to synergise his technique.

'Are you ready to come home now?'

'No.'

'Take your rightful place and power with us.'

'No.'

'You are the chosen. You can and will be Emperor.'

'No.'

'You sense it. You are the end of days, the Aharit HaYamim, the Qiyamah. The King of kings the Lord of lords. You can feel the rapture. Embrace it, envelope it. Become what you are. Remember your name, Emperor... do you remember your name? That is right Emperor... '

'STOP!'

Mister Li and the nine froze before he could pronounce my name. The boy was staring with intent, confused, not understanding what was happening. I glimpsed the future. I saw my demise. I saw their intention. I saw the battle, the plans they had for me. It could wait.

I approached the boy.

'Your mother was brave. Stupid, as you know, but very brave. She is with me now, she is happy. You will carry on your life without her. You are better off without her. Parents are overrated. You know all this.'

'Thank you, Mister Mann.'

He understood.

35

B A T L E

The boy left. I watched him disappear from sight before allowing the Xaja and Mister Li to move. It was time. They had formed the hive mind that could defeat me and I saw my fate. The strongest Xaja was channelling the energies into Mister Li, he would use the Voice to pull me into deep anger. I would take out the two weakest with an EM bomb, also most of the people in the terminal and the other Xaja shielded by Li, and the strong one. The boy would die too.

'Collateral damage,' Mister Li would later say, like so many warriors before him.

Three Xaja would rush me and occupy me with body movements, pulling me further into the carcass in martial battle. All the while Li and the others would wear me down with the Voice - causing doubts, reminding me of limitation, feeding my neurosis, making it bigger. I realised what they were doing, but too late.

In an attempt to gain control I disengage from the body and melt the minds of the three martial Xaja. I leap at Mister Li and slowly choke him. I can feel their grip diminishing; this is my only hope, to kill the conductor, the conduit.

My only hope and also exactly what they want, I felt the telltale glimmer from the deep Li mind. Yes, that's it, choke, kill with your bare hands, kill me, kill and become one of us. You have killed only by suggestion before, triggering the impulse in others' minds, hastening their desire to die or kill. But now is different, this is the point where you claim the crown, your birthright. Do it. Kill me.

Kill me.

And in that leak I saw exactly what would happen next, the power, *my* power, would drain; the remaining Xaja would take me down. Mister Li would recover and deliver the final blow. I would be captured and enslaved. Will broken, I would become part of them and be used until spent. A tortured instrument of torture. They would get the torture balance exactly right, knowing that I can resist everything, even death. The equilibrium of pleasure and pain would be exquisite. Death would never come. Ounces of pleasure with pounds, and pounds of pounding pain. Hanging. Vertical X shaped. Hairless, eyeless, finger and toe-nail-less. All my tendons cut, me bleeding slowly but sustained by a drip. Recycle the blood. Useful blood. Round and round it goes. Testicles crushed, no more covering anything or anyone in Mister Mann love.

Jaffa Cake, Mister Mann? Not for another year. Those electrodes chaffing? Well, work harder and gain control, we have wars to win, money to make, people to crush.

Earless. Noseless. Penisless. Ouch. Sure will smart a bit.

I saw this and moved. And I became everyone, woman, child and man, every animal, every thing swimming in the sea, every insect - oh the insects! I became the Xaja and Mister Li, I saw their limitations, so limited, crawling children, I saw their weakness, their death. Their death, they were so close to death, black souls, the grossest state - I knew how to kill Mister Li and the Xaja. The ecstasy was rushing through me and peace was replacing the irritating intense joy. Then a thought came, that dark, hard shiny mote. Matter resolved, action approached and I was behind them.

Pure Aikido, I moved out of the way. Three thousand, two hundred and ninety-six miles out of the way - in an instant. I teleported. They were behind me.

36

T I M E

Time is an illusion. Scientists are catching up with this. The best explanation of it is found at the excellent site *Parabrahman* where the wise man Mahatma Andy explains with skill and erudition:

'*Time is an illusion. All the clues are there. Even scientists are starting to realise. You've got to love scientists; solve one problem by coming up with ten more. Busy busy busy.* **The New Scientist** *has a good article from January 2008 called* **Is Time an Illusion?** *The best bit in the article is from the lead scientist, Carlo Rovelli:*

It is not reality that has a time flow, it is our very approximate knowledge of reality that has a time flow. Time is the effect of our ignorance.

Beautiful. Buddha could not have said it better.

Reinventing the wheel though. It has all been done before. Or as time does not exist, it has all been thought, done, improved upon instantaneously. And then redone, rethought, re-improved ad infinitum.

But even that statement implies time; but leads closer to the truth.

The concept of time is a limitation. Once you get rid of that limitation amazing things should begin to happen. Teleportation, prescience, omnipresence, you will never die and you can never be born.

Keith says that was a step too far. 'Where's the proof in the literature? At least the scientists are trying to put it in concrete terms. They are trying to understand it, you are spouting nonsense.'

I say if you get rid of another limitation, thinking, than you will be there.

Stop thinking and start experiencing.

We've all done it. Waiting for Christmas as a child. The conversations my mum had with her friends on the way to the shops, would they ever stop? Kissing my wife for the first time, seems like yesterday.

But that is not it either; those moments are again just pointers to the Truth.

Be still.

Breathe in and say to yourself 'I', breathe out and say 'Am'. Do this for a day.

I'll do it myself when I get the time. Over to Guru Adams again:

Time is an illusion. Lunchtime doubly so.
- *Douglas Adams*

There is a theory which states that if ever anybody discovers exactly what the Universe is for and why it is here, it will instantly disappear and be replaced by something even more bizarre and inexplicable. There is another theory which states that this has already happened.
- *Douglas Adams.'*

Mahatma Andy really knows what he's talking about. Often when I had doubts about the state of the world I would surf his site for inspiration. It made me realise there is goodness in this world, and people like him give us hope. He is with me now.

In reality everything happens at exactly the same moment. This is because time does not exist. Events stacked upon events, all exploding at the same moment.

Chaos.

Time is a mind construct devised to make order from the chaos. If you knew what I know you'd freak. Think of your average mundane day. Imagine all the processes of that day happening at once. Shower, shit, shave, shag - all at once. Doesn't sound too bad, but throw in work, lunch, *EastEnders*, *Coronation Street* and talking to the old lady at number five and it could get a bit embarrassing. So we stretch the events out.

If you know this you can start to control it. The beginning of omnipresence. So-called miracles begin to happen. Think about it, eliminate the constriction of time from your mind and you can be in all places at once. No time to limit your travelling. You can know everything as there is no limit on the amount of time spent learning.

Sit there in the silence with that realisation. Sit still and feel the truth between the spaces of these words.

There.

Can you feel it? Did it slip? Did time slip just for a moment?

Yes? Good.

No? Try harder.

No, that's wrong, don't try, just *do*.

And that is what I did. I teleported to the campus of Harvard, to the lecture hall of physics 101 to start up my latest campaign of freedom.

37

H A R V A R D

I practised partial omnipresence just to show Mister Li and the XAJA whores how I'd grown, how powerful I'd become. I could sense their awe and frustration. I appeared simultaneously in Paris, Cambridge, Harvard and the *Massachusetts Institute of Technology* - I chose to appear in lecture theatres. I also appeared in the Student Union at Oxford and in the library at *INSEAD*, because no one goes to lectures in either of those places.

There was no need to plant elaborate weapons or proceed through complicated initiations. Time was mastered; I had the instantaneous ability to 'recruit' to empower my soldiers, to bend their minds to do their will.

Yes, *their* will, *not* mine. They wanted to do it. It was deep within them, but most definitely there. Terrible, terrible shadows. Far worse than anything I could dream up.

Marvellous. I allowed myself a little treat. I inserted what I like to call the 'tramp chip'. In honour of my first army, in honour of Lomas, who was currently orchestrating them and getting ready for battle.

Wonderful to see an all-American prep school tosspot adopt some of the characteristics of a Glaswegian vagabond, a French lady student become slightly Irish in her ways and an over-privileged English arse become... well actually I let him become a much more amusing and sinister version of what he already was. The bad guy in American movies is always played by an English actor for very good reason.

I had ninety of the world's intellectual elite

committing heinous abominations on two continents in the style of tramps. It was a gentle piece of humour designed to let those about to die know that they should not take life too seriously. No one saw the funny side. Shame.

Why didn't you take out Reading too, Mister Mann? It's true that *Reading University* is probably the best university in the world, but it was spared because it is beautiful. The architecture, I couldn't bear for those delicate flowering 1960s buildings to be stained with blood and gore, nor see the stunted tower block Halls of Residence witness man's cruelty to man. I'm a hard man, but I am not completely without feeling. The beauty of Whiteknights, Wells, Bridges, Childs and Wessex shall remain intact. *Reading University* – a magnificent testament to an age gone by. A sleepy comforting womb of a place.

P R O S T I T U T E S

As the intellectual atrocities were precipitated another incarnation of me strode around the Campus of Whiteknights at the *University of Reading*. Taking in the majesty of the lake and striding to marvel at the red brick elegance of Bridges Hall. The winding leafy lane that bends gently to the right leads to the Quad, the senses instantly startle at the homeliness and succour of the place.

It was a terrible thing I had provoked. Violence rampaged at six universities around the world. I needed to balance the horror with beauty. And the only place that could counter the monstrous barbarity of ninety highly intelligent, creative and deeply suppressed demons was a stroll around the majesty of Bridges Hall.

I had arranged to meet a prostitute in one of the small rooms in the Halls of Residence to help me relieve the tension of this historic day.

H corridor, Room 80.

I'd also managed to persuade Monica to join us. She had never been keen on a *ménage a trois* but she knew it was important to me and acquiesced as a sign of her love. She'd got dressed up special too. The lovely red hessian dress and slutty ripped fishnet stocking number I had carefully fashioned for her for last Valentine's Day.

The professional lady remarked that it was unusual to be asked to service a man and his glove puppet, but she was more amused than scared and considered this far less offensive than some of the acts she'd been requested to perform in the past.

She offered a surprising variety of techniques and

fetishes for the hourly £150 she charged. I assured her that the water sports, coprophilia, anal play, bondage and penis torture would not be necessary and that I had no interest in being pleasured. This was Monica's time and I would be delighted if she went down on her.

'You want me to plate a puppet?'

'This is MONICA! Say hello to MONICA!' I used the Voice. She must take this seriously. She was scared now.

'Hello, Monica.'

'That's better. Do you want this job or not?'

'Yes, but it'll be three hundred an hour.'

Opportunistic bitch. So be it.

I sat in the functional chair by the bed and, with my hand up her skirt, placed Monica gently on the pillow. I worked her arms and head, beckoning the whore to get busy. My thumb pointed to the imaginary crotch and my middle finger, working the other arm, waved her in. The index finger threw the head back in anticipated resignation.

'Keep to the fabric of the dress. If your tongue touches my palm flesh the illusion will be lost. Do you understand?'

She did.

'Keep licking until Monica cums. Don't worry about the time, you'll be paid well. Is that clear?'

It was clear.

I sat in that sparse room and allowed the lady to work her charm as Monica whispered soothing sentiments in my ear. To relieve the boredom of watching a naked, busty woman perform cunnilingus on a glove puppet I allowed myself to dip in and out of the violence occurring at the other campus universities. Life and death is a timeless juxtaposition, and a beautiful aphrodisiac.

The hours went by. The prostitute started to

complain after the first thirty minutes and so unfortunately I had to enter her mind and control the action.

Lick
Violence
Lap
Gun Shots
Flick
Flutter
Bone Crack
Ripple
Dart
Blood Spray
Blood

She had been lapping at the rough hessian for over four hours now and her tongue was in shreds.

'Keep going, I think she's almost there.'

Muffled whimpers and a weak exhausted cry.

I laughed. 'Was that you Monica, or the whore?'

So, why the relationship with the hand puppet, Mister Mann? It's my way of being normal, in touch with the average person. All relationships are like mine and Monica's; one dominant sentient cunt and one inanimate taking a load of rubbish. If you think this is not true and that you love your partner and would do anything for them then, guess what, you are the puppet. If you think that the other loves you and would do anything for you then congratulations you are deluded. If you loved the other one and the other one loved you and you only lived for each other's happiness then it would be a stalemate and you'd just sit and stare into each other's eyes, each of you waiting for the other to express a want. Neither of you would move and you would die very happy, but also very soon.

There has to be a more dominant party. All relationships are 'Do what I want you to do and I'll love you. Don't do what I want you to do and I'll kill you.'

Me and Monica? We're just trying to fit in. I'm the dominant one, she is the doormat. Sometimes she gets her own way and makes my life a misery.

And so the whore moaned and passed out from tonguetacular exhaustion. Monica was almost there too. Shame. I had to finish her off myself. Quick lick of the iron-soaked hessian and a squeeze of her puppet breasts and I had her shuddering like a *Parkinson's* sufferer in an electric chair.

I paid the prostitute six times her recently upped rate and rounded it up to an Archer. She'd earned it. She'd recover from her wounds, so long as the forty notes sticking out of her mouth didn't choke her first.

I'm all heart, me.

I left my beloved *Reading University* and in an instant I was with Lomas and his tramp troops, ready to give them a lesson in teleportation.

Nothing could stop me now.

39

N I G H

The end is nigh. That's a peculiar expression. The world is an illusion, it doesn't exist. So how can it end? Nothing is going on, it just appears to be. Ask yourself the following question: 'What is my relationship to the world?'

You can't stop there, soon you're asking:

'What *is* the world?'

'What am me?'

'What am I?'

'What *is* this *I*?'

Then you'll follow the sense of I back to the source. You'll see that the I doesn't exist and what is under that is happiness, for want of a better word. In truth no word can describe it because words are inadequate.

If you think about nothing it becomes something and therefore that nothing no longer exists. It's the same thing. You can't get there. You are inadequate. All this talk about love is pointless. You can only get a facsimile of what love is like and any feeling that is not love is to some degree hate. As the limited human can never approach true love, the source of everything, all the human feeling including human love, is hate.

So why bother trying to be nice? You could try to embrace the hate but the concept of pure hate is beyond the limited human comprehension and is so awful it's fortunate we can't appreciate it. So, as all feelings that are not pure hate are to some degree, love ... Well, you can see where I'm going with this. Sometimes I think it's just me.

And so we oscillate back and forth in this world, up

and down like Bambi on roller-skates. Leave the world alone. It's a test, a proving ground and you are failing miserably. Step away from the world. You know that's the smart thing to do. And I am here to help.

Sometimes I think I'm going mad and I'm the only one who can see this. All the ungrateful people I've helped, the looks of incomprehension the moment before they die. No tributes. It would be nice to be appreciated just the once.

There I go again, wanting approval. Silly Mister Mann getting caught up in the illusion of the world.

I had a choice; I could have followed the path of love, humility and compassion like so many sages and saints before me. None of this is new, it is all written in the scriptures, you only have to look. Jesus, Buddha and the other one. Babaji, Yogananda, Saint Cyril of Scilly. It's a well-trod path. I could have preached the truth their way. But where did it get them? Crucified, vilified, their words, distorted and twisted to propagate man's inhumanity to man. No, better to go straight to the source. I'm not a messiah who shows love, humility and compassion. I'm a messiah who doesn't give a fuck. I don't care what you think or think that you think. I'm going to tell you straight, go to the source, and show you the horrors you create, no long-winded gentle reincarnation until realisation for you. I don't believe in reincarnation anyway, and I didn't the first time I was here. Reincarnation like scientific doctrine is just a concept. Concepts are lies. It is all an illusion. Let go. It doesn't work; it is too drawn out, taking millions of years.

This is the fast track.

This is light speed Zionism.

Buddha Express.

Choo Choo Jew.

I'm going to deliver, going to get you there fast.

This is the end of days.

The cataclysm that will take you all home, and me with you.

Lomas had recruited and trained (by pyramid scheme) over a million wasters. He had stamped his own personality on his army and I approved.

'Every army needs a uniform. It is tradition,' he stated. Khaki's been done to death, blue-grey, green they're all so last war. The religions of the world had exhausted all the bright colour combos.

Lomas favoured an insect motif and I thought it fitting as humans would soon be demonstrating the hive mind. Wasps, he loved wasps and he had cultivated a lovely wasp beard and side-burns. The insects under his control formed an immaculate face piece that was so convincing only the buzzing gave it away.

His army sported yellow and black jump suits with big insect-eye sun glasses by *Prada*. Very smart. Very unnerving. Lomas had a gift for the dramatic. If I believed in the world I'd almost say we were brothers. But I know that I am you, I am everyone and everything. Lomas was not my sibling, but me.

40

H I V E

Most people baulk at the idea of humans having a hive mind, a universal consciousness. That's because they want to be individuals, they want an ego, they want to be different. They want to be so different that they all buy the same brand clothing, similar newspapers; they eat at themed restaurant chains, holiday in traditional styles. It was a genius of Lomas to stick a nice big *Prada* on those sunglasses to reinforce the point.

Uniforms, suit and tie, even Dress Down Friday has a uniform; blue shirt and chinos for the men, slutty dresses for the ladies. Even the ones that rebel against the rules have a uniform: ripped jeans, or shorts and sandals - how terribly original.

Conformity is the most obvious example of the hive mind in action. Trying to fit like a social insect. The ant building bridges and cooperating, foraging for food. The bee, anything for the queen. Mole rats, lemmings, we humans are no different, except that our hive mind goes a lot deeper. Still, we all have the same thoughts, dreams, desires, fears and angers. We are all so predictably the same. The ultimate predator, the top of the food chain, we can take on any species on this planet, including our own, and annihilate it.

Don't fuck with us.

For every human killed by a shark we have killed six million of them. Stupid animal still hasn't learnt.

We are barbaric as a race. For pleasure we go to a restaurant and order a nice juicy steak. How would you like it, sir? The convention is the rarer the better. Take the horns off, wipe its arse and serve it up. The Spanish like to bull fight on the plate, that's how rare they like it. Some restaurants are now serving fresh fish: fish caught, cooked, dying, dead and eaten on the table.

Is this necessary?

Geese force fed to fatten the liver, then slaughtered at table so their engorged organs can be enjoyed at goose body temperature.

Barbaric.

Even a cunt like Hitler was vegetarian. If he got it, why don't you?

With the choice western society offers we should all be vegetarian. Fresh vibrant vegetables or pain-drenched meat? Your body is not a graveyard yet you fill it, and fuel it, with the fear-infused flesh of dead animals. And this is one of the reasons you have dark thoughts; you want power, dominion over the beasts, including those of your own race.

When a man walks down a street behind a good-looking woman who limps slightly, he thinks dark thoughts.

'Why not? I've just devoured the flesh of a defenceless animal, killed for no reason whatsoever, I might as well.'

He senses her vulnerability and thinks about giving in to his beast side, about tripping her up, filling her arse with his spunk. He feels a bit guilty for thinking like that but then justifies it. It's simply his way of sharing the defenceless animal protein that he has just senselessly devoured. Two wrongs do not make a right.

They're just thoughts, Mister Mann, we don't actually do those things.

Be careful with those thoughts.

I'm only speaking for a man here. I have no idea about women. I reckon they are far crueller. A woman might see a nice-looking man and think 'I'd like to split your penis open with a sharp knife, turn it inside out and make a vagina from it, shove a bowling ball up there and challenge you to force it out. And then maybe I'll let you get me pregnant - you dreamy, tight-bunned hunk of a man, you!'

Who knows what women think?

Thoughts relate to actions and are a slippery slope. You want a new pair of curtains but can't afford them, so you wish your parents dead.

Oh, but I can't think that! It might happen and that would be terrible. But I'd get some curtains with the inheritance and probably a house so it wouldn't be *too* bad. But that's appalling; I don't really want Mum and Dad to die.

Don't you? *You* thought it. Be careful with those thoughts. You are the creator of your world. Look around you. All and everything is due to your thoughts and your actions. Well done.

The effortless thought is subtle. Too strong and you will reverse it, natural resistance to everything. The thought must be like a shadow, no, a reflection of a shadow, or even a picture of a shadow reflected in the shadow of a reflection. Subtle. And then you can create anything and everything.

But, you sit there thinking dark thoughts and beating yourself up for having these bad thoughts. And you say no one has these thoughts like you, but again you are deceived. Everyone has thoughts exactly like you. You don't stand a chance; you were born to think them. It was preordained. It's called conditioning. Everyone thinking the same thoughts, an out of step and dis-configured hive mind. It will be my pleasure to bring everyone into step to unify the hive... and get you all thinking of the ultimate.

Death.

41

D E A T H

There are so many ways to die. I have experienced death many times. I have persuaded many people to die, I've been inside their minds and experienced a variety of deaths.

Death is not as bad as it sounds. Not if you know what to expect. It is the fear of dying that's terrifying. Once you have conquered that you have conquered everything.

Death occurs when the supply of freshly oxygenated blood to the brain is cut off. Ten seconds before you're unconscious. Very few use those seconds wisely. Most panic. Occasionally someone will sit back and be the observer to the experience.

There are many things that prevent oxygen reaching the brain.

Drowning is a classic, mainly because it is so dramatic, with several phases of panic. It is neither pretty nor painless, as so many romantic novels suggest. Fifty-five percent of death by drowning incidents occur three meters from safety, and two thirds of the people that find themselves in trouble are good swimmers. This, of course, is accidental drowning. When I'm involved then it doesn't matter if they can swim or not. And, with regard to the proximity of safety, it's a moot point. The surface struggle is where the victim realises he is drowning and climbs an imaginary ladder out of the water to try to get air.

PANIC

This panic will last twenty to seventy seconds. Gulping then going under several times.

PANIC

Struggling to breathe, they can't call for help.

PANIC

In the end they lose all strength, stop struggling and take a final breath - which they can hold from between twenty and one hundred seconds. All the while, panicking.

Then the painful bit begins, they inhale some water.

PANIC

Spluttering, coughing, inhaling more water. A reflex laryngospasm occurs, sealing shut the airways. The feeling is of burning and tearing flesh in the chest as the water pours down. And then... there may be a two second feeling of calmness and tranquillity, representing the beginnings of loss of consciousness from oxygen deprivation. Heart stops, brain dies.

Drowning can be quick, especially if the water is cold:

Average drowning time - approximately two panic-stricken minutes. Not a nice way to go. But if you sit back and detach yourself from the unusualness and pain it's not too bad. If only people didn't panic it would be a much more enjoyable experience.

So what about a heart attack? That any better? Yes. The film style heart attack - clutching the chest, flailing, desperate chronic pain and immediate collapse – that does happen but is not common. Typically, a myocardial infarction is a lot less dramatic. Chest pain is the most common symptom, tightness or squeezing. Pain will radiate to the jaw, throat, back, stomach and arms. Shortness of breath, nausea and cold sweats. All due to the heart muscle struggling and dying. Some heart attacks can feel like indigestion, tiredness or cramps. But even these mild arrests can play havoc with the electrical impulses that control the heart muscle contractions and cause the heart to stop. Ten seconds later the person is unconscious. Minutes later they are dead. Not my favourite way to die. Too quick, and not enough emotional play.

Bleeding to death, now that's a man's way to go:

This can be very quick, seconds, if the aorta, the major blood vessel leading to the heart, is severed. This can happen after a severe fall or car accident. Exsanguinations can last for hours, then the various stages of haemorrhagic shock. A main artery is severed. The average adult has five litres of blood. You can lose up to seven hundred and fifty millilitres without too many symptoms. At one and a half litres you'll begin to feel weak, anxious and a little thirsty.

Thirst is the body's way of telling you that you are losing liquid. At two litres you'll be dazed and confused. Most would be in fear at this stage. If you are strong you can overcome these emotions and watch the exquisite ebb of your life force slide into the unconsciousness.

Wonderful. All this will depend largely on the extent of your wounds. A single penetrating wound to the femoral artery in the leg will be a lot easier to cope with than the pain from multiple fractures sustained during the mangling from a torturer.

Talking of torture, burning to death is very nasty if you cannot transcend the primitive emotions of terror, and if you associate too much with your body. Then the burning will trigger a rapid inflammatory response, which boosts sensitivity to the injured tissues and surrounding areas. Agony. Burns inflict intense and immediate pain through the nociceptors, the pain nerves in the skin. Third degree burns don't hurt as much as second degree burns, as these superficial nerves are destroyed, but the difference is minor and largely semantic, burns are horrifically painful.

Exquisite, makes you feel alive.

And then there is the smell of burning flesh, the singed hair and eyebrows, the scorch of hot air in the throat and airways making breathing difficult... and eventually impossible.

I burned to death once. In the early days before I'd fully mastered control of the body. I remember longing for the quick release of decapitation.

Beheading can be nearly instantaneous if done correctly and is one of the least painful ways to die. And it looks good. Gruesomely dramatic. Consciousness does continue after the spinal cord is severed - about seven seconds for a healthy, robust human not prone to fainting fits. So, you can actually view your body twitching in the middle of the room as your head rolls to the corner.

Electrocution is another quickie: The heart and the brain are the most vulnerable organs. The 'accidental' electrocutions I have arranged involved low, household currents, the most common cause of death is arrhythmia, stopping of the heart. Unconsciousness then occurs after the standard ten seconds.

Higher voltages are meant to produce near immediate death. That's the theory with the electric chair. The electrodes attached to the head are supposed to pass a powerful surge through the brain and knock the victim unconscious immediately. But the thick skull bone is such a good insulator it prevents sufficient current from reaching the brain, the skull however heats up and subsequently the brain boils.

Actual cause of death? Suffocation due to paralysis of the breathing muscles.

Very unpleasant.

F
A
L
L
I
N
G from heights is reasonably quick and was the method I preferred in the early days.

The grace.

Terminal velocity is two hundred kilometres per hour and is achieved after falling one hundred and forty-five metres.

Most people fell from shorter distances.

Seventy-five percent of the victims died within a few seconds or minutes of landing.

Hitting the ground at speed would invariably cause either:

- crushed and collapsed lungs
- exploding hearts
- damage to major arteries
- shattered ribs and bones
- some or all of the above

Hanging is another dramatic one, and its success depends largely on the victim's skill with a rope.

The rope puts pressure on the windpipe and the arteries that lead to the brain.

Done right, you're out in ten seconds, but if the noose is incorrectly sited you end up dancing, struggling violently with pain and it'll take fifteen minutes or more until asphyxiation.

I'd usually go for the

.

.

.

short drop hanging to break the neck as well. Occasionally, though space considerations allowing, I'd encourage a

.

.

.

.

.

.

.

long drop off the side of a bridge, so the victim could reach a speed that would rip the head clean off. Nice and quick, I'm all heart, me.

The US government approved lethal injection is an interesting one. It is three injections. First thiopental, an anaesthetic to take away the feeling of pain. Then a paralytic agent called pancuronium to stop the breathing. The last injection is potassium chloride which stops the heart instantly. That is the idea anyway and it's hailed as being painless and humane. What actually happens is that the drug doses get messed up, sometimes deliberately, to ensure a very nasty death. The anaesthetic is usually omitted so the victim can feel the convulsing, heaving searing pain caused by the potassium chloride. Usually the paralytic drug is sufficient to quash the condemned's ability to show signs of pain and give the game away, but occasionally one will sit up and scream.

So, dying is all about lack of oxygen to the brain. How you die can be a combination of the all the above, and other more macabre inventions. Burning, whilst falling, skinned alive, bleeding from a major artery, whilst pumped full of potassium chloride. You get the idea and I am sure you can think of many other ways to die. Give it a go and experience how liberating it is. Imagine yourself dying these ways. Lie naked on a bed, arms and legs splayed out and imagine being stabbed to death, or skinned alive, or rats eating bits of your body or birds plucking your eyes from your head and you dying slowly from the wounds. Get involved, confront that fear of dying.

I would spend days musing about the different ways I could die, so that when I caused the train event I could hold my head high and say I'd been there. I wouldn't ask of anyone any thing I had not already asked of myself. To get the fear up and out I would dream about being gang-raped on the train, abused by the hoards of passengers, chained to the balance bars over several days, buggered repeatedly by commuters that have had a bad day. I would often end up dying at the hands of a mousey librarian who over extends herself with a dildo because of a late return repeat offender.

The worse way to die is to live. Ounces of pleasure for pounds of pain. The cruellest torture of them all. What if you cannot die? Then what? There should be no problem. Enjoy it. For the Truth is you cannot die. You were never born. You are unborn. You do not exist and you do not prevail. So relax about death, it is not bad at all.

I don't know why I bother trying to explain it. It's all so ridiculous because no matter how much I show you people, you still make things worse. You still get caught up in your petty worlds striving for success. Stamping on each other, scrabbling to succeed. Look at the language of business:

Kill or be killed.

They're just words, Mister Mann.

Are they? Sounds like thought to me. And from thoughts stem ideas and then actions and then results. Animals.

I haven't killed anyone I've merely suggested you do it yourself. I'm a messiah for the common man. Jesus, Buddha *et al* were messiahs for nice people. There aren't many of them around so I want to make you realise, I want to help more people than they did. Buddha did it for himself. Jesus died once for our sins. Me, I'm all heart, I've died thousands of times, in your mind, as the last moments of life slip away. Don't get me wrong, it was no chore. I quite enjoy it. Fascinating, really. And I want to help as many of you as I can. That doesn't make me better than Jesus or the others, just different. They chose a more subtle way. I chose a direct way. I'm a messiah for cunts. I use the term cunt here, and not in the friendly old cockney grandpa greeting his grandson way. 'Hello you little cunt, come in and have a cuppa.' No, I use it in the way Al Pacino used it in the film *Glengarry Glen Ross*. Proper CUNTS.

You don't die anyway. Because the world is an illusion. Absolute truth never changes. It can't, it's the truth. So anything that changes is a lie.

The world changes, it's a lie, your body changes, it's a lie, your mind changes, it's a lie. You are a lie, an illusion. Wake up.

So, no one dies. You just imagine it. And you imagine it in horrible ways. The hive mind knows all about the concentration camps of the World War II. Oh it loves that one, revelling in the horror. If you don't like it, stop thinking about it. But you secretly like it. It's titillating. You love to talk about it and agree it was a terrible thing. And we should carry on making documentaries and harrowing pain-condensed films lest we forget. And it happens again, over and over again. What a surprise. Yeah right. It will never happen if no one thinks about it.

Wake up!

Careful, Mister Mann with that persuasive argument. The Jews won't like it and they will come to get you like they did the good lord Jesus. You know the Christ killers won't think twice about you because you appear to be actually evil. Fuck the Jews and the Arabs and the Americans and the Christians and everybody who can't see that this whole world is just one great big fucked up glorious illusion. You are shocked by these words? More shocked by them than by what man has done to man in the past; the pogroms, the concentration camps, the Aborigine genocide, the torture, the government lies, the brainwashing and what man continues to do today? Fuck them all. It might wake them up; a large portion of Mister Mann love might rouse them from their stupors. Fuck them all. Every cunt needs a good fucking. That's what they are for. Simple utility.

So wake up and be happy. You don't die. Nothing can hurt you unless of course you want it to.

You deviant fucks.

GERRARD G. GERRARD

42

C O M E D Y

Death is funny. Dave Allen, Harold Lloyd, Laurel and Hardy - all the greats have mocked it.

I've noticed lately that comedy has become more brutal. Visceral hatred, racism disguised as ridiculous ignorance. Homophobia disguised as just a bit of fun. Sexism disguised as nice tits, luv. Sniping, astringent, personal, attacking comedy. Edgy. Is it funny, you ask? You're not sure but everyone else is laughing, so it must be. And you recite the catchphrases to fit in. Really cruel comedians, crude comedians, smug-self-satisfied-intellectual-snob comedians, not-at-all-funny comedians, look-at-me-I'm-fat comedians.

'I caught my wife turkey basting the spunk from my wanking sock the other day. I think she wants another baby.'

How is that funny?

I long for the halcyon days of comedy. Gentle, skilled comedy, reliant on timing and the *mot juste*. Morecambe and Wise, Gerard Hoffnung, Frank Muir and Arthur Marshall on *Call My Bluff*. Willie Rushton and Tim Brooke-Taylor on *I'm Sorry I Haven't a Clue*. A bit of Barry Took or Joan Sims. Kenneth Williams sucking on a double entendre. Ronnie Barker and Harry Worth. George Formby, Victoria Wood, Bernard Bresslaw, Norman Wisdom or a Rossiter. Oh Leonard, oh Frankie, oh Flanders and Swann! Joyce Grenfell, Margaret Rutherford and Maureen Lipman!

I decided to redress the balance. Another television show? No. I'm going straight to the top. The hardest gig of them all. Stand up. In the best place in the world to perform. *The Comedy Store*, Oxendon Street, London. Bit of a risk.

Television you can edit. With stand up you have to be note perfect, timing immaculate. The pauses, the looks, the body language just right. One slip, one nervous twitch, or slightly out of pitch voice and the crowd would turn. They'll have you. One of you, three hundred and fifty of them. Would I die on stage or would I kill them?

I killed them.

I took to the stage on a Thursday night on one of the try out spots in the second half. I was on just before the main event, the headline comedian. I felt sorry for him as I knew I would upstage him and have the audience dying with laughter. When I'd finished with them there would be little point him going on. The audience would be spent. Nothing could top my act.

'Good evening, my name is Mister Mann. Good clean humour. No swearing and I'd appreciate it if no one heckles.'

A man in the audience heckles on cue.

'You're rubbish, mate.'

'SHUT THE FUCK UP, CUNT!' Full Voice directed at the man. He slumps in the chair and dies. The audience laughs, not knowing the man is dead. Nothing gets the audience on your side quite like a display of raw man-destroying power. Those around the dead man, nervous about his slouched form and bleeding ears, are quickly controlled. They sit and pay attention.

'What did the snail say when riding on the tortoise's back?'

'Weeeee!'

The laughter died down at the joke. I shrugged and moved swiftly on.

'What happens when you cross a Great White with a

cow? I don't know but I wouldn't want to milk it.'

Quiet room, a few groans, they've heard these before.

'What did the number one say to the number eight?'
'Nice belt!'

Groans, a boo. Shuffling nervousness. They really haven't seen anything like this since they were eight years old in assembly, and jokes were delivered by the boy in the Harrington jacket who thought he was cool.

'Knock, knock!'

A few people encouraging me politely reply with the traditional 'Who's there?' The rest stare in disgust and the chit-chat level rises. I am dying on my feet, just as I planned.

'Who's there?'

'Panther.'

No one bothers to join in so I answer myself.

'Panther who? 'Panther or no panther, I'm going thwimming!'

Silence.

'Is it the way I tell 'em?'

'Yes, you're shit, mate!'

'It's not the way I tell 'em,' I tell them, 'it's the way you're listening to them. Why do you not take responsibility and learn to enjoy yourselves?'

The crowd sense a victim and the egos join together and show disapproval.

'Get off!'

'Rubbish!'

'You're shit, get off!'

I let them heckle, gently probing their minds, encouraging them to braver insults, feeding the pack. They want blood; they start to enjoy picking on the victim, the lone man at the front trying to entertain.

Who does he think he is?

It's our duty to tell him he's shit, no constructive criticism, he needs to be told directly and bluntly, crushed, destroyed, he's wasting our time.

Who told him he was funny?

He must die.

We are three hundred and fifty strong, he is one, we will tear him apart.

That hive mind forming the pack.

'Get off!' 'You're rubbish.' 'You stink.' 'Your mum's a cunt.' 'You're ugly.' 'Get a haircut.'

I let them go, persuading them higher. The bouncers look nervous, sensing the mob, one gestures to me to get off, if I know what's good for me. The red light goes on; the management want me to leave. A bouncer moves to protect me and usher me off stage.

A glass is thrown. The bouncer prevents the large thug who is now on stage from punching me.

'STOP!'

The room is under Mister Mann control.

'Return to your seat, young man, and I will help you appreciate the humour behind my jokes.'

The lumpen complies. Silence fills the room. The bouncer recedes.

'Why was 6 afraid of 7? Because 7-8-9!'

First a titter, then a giggle, a slight chortle. That's enough. Silence returns.

'Knock, knock!'

'Who's there?' They all enthusiastically enquire.

'Interrupting cow.'

'Interrupting cow wh… '

'Mooooo!'

A snort, building to a laugh, then a snicker. Stop. Silence returns. I leave the stage and approach a woman in the front row. 'Knock, knock!' I say to her and immediately place the microphone to her mouth. I allow her to speak. 'Who's there?' she asks cheerfully.

'Interrupting starfish.'

'Interrupting starfish wh… '

I splay my hand to resemble a starfish, cover her mouth and hold it there.

The crowd laughs, then a shriek, a howl, and a whoop. Stop.

Silence. I remove my hand and calmly return to the stage.

'What did the Zen Buddhist say to the hotdog vendor?'

'We don't know, what *did* the Zen Buddhist say to the hotdog vendor?'

'Make me one with everything.'

Laughter, a shriek, building to scream and turning down to a low 'oh dear'. More laughter, I let it go.

'A man walks into a library and says, 'Hi, I'd like a cheeseburger.' The librarian says, 'This is a library.' The man says (whisper), 'I'd like a cheeseburger.'

The laughter builds louder, a few tears, heads start to ache with the exercised face muscles.

'What do you get if you cross a toad with a galaxy? Star warts.'

Guffaws, howl, snicker, chortle, shrieks, whoops, tears. Pounding aching backs of heads.

'I can't tell putty from toothpaste. My windows fell out.'

Bursts, laughs, break ups, chuckles, giggles, grinning, snorts, roars.

'What's a foot long and slippery? A slipper.'

Cackles, screams, titters, laughs, belly laughs. Oh my head really hurts.

'What's green and sings? Elvis Parsley.'

The volume of mirth in the room becomes quite deafening, ears begin to bleed.

'Knock, knock!'

'Who's there?'

'Banana.'

'Banana who?'

'Knock, knock!'

'Who's there?'

'Banana.'

'Banana who?'

'Knock, knock!'

'Who's there?'

'Banana.'

'Banana who?'

'Knock, knock!'

'Who's there?'

'Orange.'

'Orange who?'

'Orange you glad I didn't say banana?'

That one got them. A few started to roll in the aisles. They didn't roll very much because they were dead. Brain haemorrhage. I was killing them.

'Knock, knock!'

'Who's there?'

'Control freak. Now you say, 'Control freak who?'

They saw the irony of that one. That was the best reaction so far. Gasping for air. Howls and whoops. Heads really hurting.

'A guy and gal go on date to Trattoria, an Italian restaurant. It's important you remember what type of restaurant, because that plays large in this joke. It's also important for you to know that cannelloni is a pasta dish, which is Italian. They arrive, they order and she disappears to powder her nose. He waits ten minutes... He waits twenty minutes... He waits half an hour! Will she ever return? He sighs. When she eventually comes back, the food has arrived and he's playing with the pasta, swirling it about with his fingers. 'What on earth do you think you are doing?' she screams in disgust. 'I was just feeling cannelloni.''

Raucous deafening laughter.

'You really are too kind, I told that last one really badly. Please, you're humouring me.'

The merriment continued.

'I've got you now, it doesn't really matter what I say. You are allowing yourself to be free. Viewed in the right way anything can be funny. Even death.'

The laughter dies down as more people become free and die.

'My dog has no nose.'

'Your dog has no nose?'

'Nope, no nose.'

'How does he smell?'

'He can't; he has no nose!'

Less laughter as more people join me.

'This guy walks into a bar with a chicken and an alligator. The guy says to the bartender, 'I'll have a Scotch and soda.' The alligator says, 'I'll have a Martini.' 'That's amazing,' says the bartender, 'that alligator can talk!' 'Actually,' says the guy, 'I'm a ventriloquist.''

Just three people struggling to laugh, the room becoming quite still.

'Why did the chicken cross the road? I don't know.'

A whimper.

'Knock, knock! Come in.'

A murmur.

'How is a chicken different from an Israeli-Palestinian peace agreement? One is a domestic fowl; the other is a treaty.'

They are almost still now.

'A comedy audience goes to the doctors dying with laughter and the doctor says, 'Well audience, it's not good news. You don't have much time left.' 'Oh God!' the audience says. 'How long do we have?' 'Ten,' says the doc. 'Ten? Ten what? Years? Months? What, doc?

'Nine. Eight...

'Three. Two. One. Thank you, and goodnight.'

Silence.

Silence. Stillness. The power of comedy. All three hundred and fifty dead.

I laugh.

I killed them.

43

B E A U T Y

Beauty is only skin deep unless you are into veins, subcutaneous tissue and bleeding organs. I suppose what I am trying to say is that beauty is subjective. There is a common agreement of what constitutes great beauty but most of that agreement in the west is formed by the brainwashing media and peer pressure. It is ludicrous what constitutes great beauty today. It has changed so much over the years. Women used to be plump and rounded now they are stick thin, resemble boys and appeal largely to homosexuals. But as homosexuals govern the fashion industry and the fashion industry dictates how the majority of people think and act then most people view skeletons as sexy. But deep down they don't. Deep down they don't want perfect fragrant skin and bones; they want something with a bit of flesh on it, unkempt, kicking up a bit of a whiff, something that reminds them of their unwashed childhoods.

And on the subject of smells, most high end perfume is made from whale vomit. Ambergris is sperm whale puke. It is usually found floating on the sea or washed ashore in large lumps weighing up to fifty kilograms. Fresh whale vomit actually has a strong faecal smell. But after years of photo-degradation and oxidation in the ocean it takes on a sweet, earthy, animal, marine quality that is not unlike isopropanol but without the astringent harshness. Similarly Eau de Mann, my own brand of homemade scent, starts out with a smell that is a mixture of excrement, spunk, spit, urine, blood and very carroty vomit but soon matures over a few years degrading in the seasons to a musty, heady olfaction of sweet, earthy, musk tones with a hint of bergamot. The ladies go wild for it. And so they should, I put a lot of 'Me' into that creation.

Ambergris, the whale chunder, fetches ten dollars per gram or higher depending on the quality of the regurgitation. Eau de Mann is priceless and not for sale.

Ambergris is put to other uses: as incense, as a means to scent cigarettes and as a flavouring for food. It is considered an aphrodisiac. It is also used as a medicine for headaches, colds, epilepsy and other ailments. Ambergris is also moulded, dried, decorated and worn as jewellery. I might be tempted to try Eau de Mann in those applications. Jelly jewellery for Monica, a nice pearl necklace.

And on the subject of bile, what about honey? Bee barf: lovely on toast or in a nice cup of tea. Sticky, sweet nectar, but still sick. You see, people can be so precious about what they eat, smell or wear but they are hypocrites; recoiling at the suggestion that they are in fact partial to a bit of vomit.

And so, to the beauty of sight, taste and smell. What we find desirable is in fact repulsive. Wake up. Look around, think about what you do. And the last two of the five gross senses, touch and hearing, what beauty lies there? Only five senses, you see how limited we are? The range of electromagnetic radiation an eye can sense is so minute compared to the vastness out there, picking up only a fraction of the vibration available. Smell, touch, taste, hearing too. Hearing ; have you seen *The X-Factor*, have you listened, can they sing? Compared to a whale or a dolphin, they cannot. Compare the wannabes' song to the distilled classics of Beethoven the Plagiarist, they cannot engender anything like the same heraldic reaction.

And compared to the symphony of the cosmos that I

hear constantly, Beethoven is a mere childish kazoo player. Release your gross senses and expand into the universe and experience what is available. What is available? I cannot describe it, as words are limited and produce only concepts. Can you describe the taste of an orange so the listener knows exactly its flavour? No. You must experience it. Be not in the world. Drop the illusion. Stop limiting yourself. Beauty really is only very wafer thin, skin deep, there is so much more just below the surface of the illusion you call the world.

44

K N O W L E D G E

There is only one thing I hate more than quotes from famous people and that is people who quote quotes from famous people. Quotes and words of wisdom are useless. Take for example this one from Thomas A. Edison: We don't know a millionth of one percent about anything.

The A in Thomas A. Edison clearly stands for Arse. What does he know? We know everything but we have forgotten, we choose not to remember.

People use this statement and laugh knowingly.

'Are we not big that we can laugh at ourselves in such a self-deprecating but clever manner; using the supposed wisdom of a supposed genius to illustrate the point that we are just infants in knowledge, learning to crawl?'

'I am using this statement to say I know nothing but it makes me cleverer than the rest because at least I realise I don't know.'

The lunacy is that we know everything; we are everything, if only we stop pretending and start to remember. Self-deprecating? Self-defecating.

And whoever said 'Wise men make proverbs, but fools repeat them' is an idiot. Every quote ever uttered can be proven to be useless. A quote is a concept and therefore a thing of limitation. It is redundant. Words are useless, except maybe the words you read now, because at least these may provoke you into getting your head removed from your rectum.

This is the only quote of any use:

'You are a cunt.' – *Mister Mann*.

That is the only piece of deep wisdom man needs. If only you would ponder that statement deeply. Read it and reread it until you understand that you really are a cunt and everyone you meet is a cunt too. Everyone you know is a prize cunt. If they weren't they would not be on this earth. Ponder the message. Have it scrolling as screensaver. Have a little *Post-It* note stuck on your bathroom mirror with 'You are a cunt' written on it. To remind you. Set an alarm every hour of the day to remind you that you are a cunt. Ponder, reflect and digest till you know that you are a cunt. And when the realisation strikes then you have two options:

1. To carry on being a cunt
2. Do something about it

Those are the only real choices you have in life.

God, I should go into the self help business. This is pure gold.

45

T R A M P D O M

Thy Trampdom come, thy will be done.

They congregated in Docklands, at the disused and monumental Millennium building. Docklands: a beautiful wasteland of failed ambition and struggling beauty. I had assembled an army of approximately twenty-four thousand of the strongest of my recruits in the main vaulted turbine room of the Millennium Mills building. I was in the middle. To the North - Lomas in his splendid insect uniform. Absolute silence except for the faint hum of his beard. Only five minds active, the sixth hive mind silent and waiting.

Lomas had six thousand strong recruits amassed in his quadrant of the auditorium. His mind laughed; he understood it was all a game.

To the East, looking reluctant in the Lomas- designed uniform, was Morgan with the six thousand in his quadrant. He wasn't one for ceremony and conformity and was itching to get started, every fibre of his being cried, 'Cut the crap!' Such anger, such rage. He reminded me of me as a young man. Perfect, he understood it was no joke and that the game had to be won at all costs.

To the South stood Varcoe heading his army of six thousand in that quarter. If Lomas was the creativity and Morgan the raw power, then Varcoe was the detail. He would control the hive and understand every single mind straining to pull free of the unity. He rested in nonchalance, liking the exquisite stitching of the uniform, but secretly wishing he could change the overly fussy epaulets and replace the solid gold buttons with platinum, a far more expensive and industrially useful metal.

Finally, to the West: The young Gouge. I needed him to anchor the living machine. Things would soon become trippy. Unbelievable. And the tendency to transcend would be enormous. We needed Gouge's young lust and pride, his hunger for change; we needed his anger at the world to keep us in the world. The six thousand behind him shared his qualities, just as the other quarters mirrored their leaders.

I attuned my mind to the cosmic symphony. The noise that has been called:

> Om
>
> Aum
>
> Amen

I let it vibrate in the air, the low oceanic roar mounting. The symphony the ocean, the living machine in this building a mere wavelet on that ocean. Forty-two other such machines in major cities around the world all started up at exactly the same moment. One million, eight thousand, one hundred and sixty-nine components became as one. One machine-being existed.

I allowed the Aum to fill the room, and channelled the Amen to the other forty-two chambers around the world. The Om resonated. The no-sound built. The ocean thundered in the minds of the individuals, which became the cells of the whole. To an observer outside the hive the rooms were completely silent, the deafening silence you hear at night in a forest recently purged by fire. The power surged, the energy pulsed, the force flowed. Then I released and they were gone. All one million, eight thousand, one hundred and sixty-eight disappeared. All, one, gone. The rooms filled with the noise of emptiness.

I stood alone in the Millennium building.

It was done.

46

E U L O G Y

While I waited for Mister Li to come I decided to amuse myself. Bored with ringing the *Samaritans* I indulged my other hobbies.

'Frank was a good man, but like everyone, he had problems.' The church was full and the congregation looked at me expectantly.

'A good life, a full life, and it was fuller than you might imagine.' I let a wry grin form at the side of my mouth to relieve the tension of the moment. Some people chuckled nervously as they remembered Frank's more colourful side.

'A man can get up to a lot in eighty-six years and Frank got up to a lot. He would often be seen waving at youngsters and encouraging them to cheer and shout as he showed his belly. Apparently, we must be thankful; because rumour has it as a youth he would proffer another part of his anatomy!'

Just the right amount of Voice to engender a feeling of playful *bonhomie*. Laughter.

'He was a keen gardener, was Frank, spent a lot of his time in his shed, some say to get a little peace and quiet. God knows we can all use that sometimes.'

More nods of agreement and disapproving, yet understanding, frowns from others.

'But Frank had a secret that none of you here know about.'

Extreme Eulogy was a favourite hobby. I'd endear myself to

the family of the deceased, posing as a very good friend of the departed, then I'd suggest I should read the eulogy. Such times are distressing and trying, after all. In the beginning, in the early days as a callow youth, I would make up any old shit. Then, as I matured I found it was easy to unearth actual horrible truths. Suspicions in the minds of the surviving family and friends, combined with the results of my rudimentary detective work around the house and in local newspapers. I would usually start with some standard pre-prepared sanitary summary of the departed's life but always end with a marvellous rancid revelation.

There are standard common skeletons in most people's closets. Boring. To keep my interest from waning a certain amount of surveillance work was necessary, but it was worth the effort. By such means I'd discover, for example, a particularly marvellous pervert. Frank was one such deviant.

'Frank doesn't mind you all knowing now. He has given up his body and realises his folly. He would have told you himself, now that he acknowledges there is nothing real in the world. But at the time of living he was exactly like you and believed implicitly in this illusion, this fantastically persistent illusion called the world.'

I was losing a few here. Regain their attention by asking a question.

'What do you think he got up to in that shed? What did he really do in that shed?'

Uncomfortable shifting. Time for a subtle bit of control. Not too much. The rawest reactions are the best.

'OK. I wonder if Doris, Frank's lovely and faithful wife, ever told you what she found in a secret compartment in that shed: A churchwarden pipe, a pouch of tobacco and a stash of mediocre seventies pornographic magazines. So?

What's wrong with that? Who amongst us hasn't looked at mucky pictures whilst sucking on a churchwarden charged with the finest Virginian shag, eh vicar?'

Outrage.

'No, I'm talking of a bigger secret.'

Shock.

'Hush, calm down or I won't tell you.' Gentle persuasion, order resumes.

'Old seventies pornographic magazines were the clue. Why wasn't he treating his long tall gentleman in the pink polar neck jumper to *New Scientist* and *National Geographic*, the more usual reading material of the geriatric jodder? Because, ladies and gentleman, that stash was a decoy used to hide a larger secret. Underneath that compartment was another more copious space containing the paraphernalia of his perversion. Frank had taken masturbation to a different level.'

Tension building…

OUTRAGE

More control. Simmer audience, simmer, don't boil yet.

'Several mangy examples of taxidermy; a badger, a small shrew and an egret. One Polaroid camera. A handful of stained Polaroid snaps of Frank himself - naked. And of course the elusive copies of New Scientist, including a nano-tech special, most of the pages stuck together, only the Professor Hawking interview left unsullied.'

Interest, quizzical looks. Murderous rage, simmering.

'Out of respect for the dead I won't describe the photos of Frank, but I should add that he stretched himself to the limits to accommodate that badger. But why am I telling you this? Why am I not delivering a more usual eulogy, explaining how Frank was the very model of a decent citizen who fought in World War II, and contributed much-needed help to the local church? Because, my friends, life is futile. It is over in the blink of a tired eye.

Here is the truth: when your body dies your sense of individuality, your ego, your presence and your being go into oblivion, all that you think you are is entirely obliterated. Gone forever. No one remembers you, because in reality there is no one. Only the Absolute remains. You are not this body mind, so you know no death, only the disappearance of your personality. So realise your relevance, before you irrelevantly depart. Life is a lie. Including all that I have told you. It does not exist. It is a paradox, a paradox you have to experience, so wake up and do something about it. Time is running out.

'What Frank created in these photos has as much relevance as anything else, he should be applauded for his creativity and the boundaries he was willing to push in order to improve his bodily awareness. Let us not see this feat go unmentioned. Ladies and gentlemen, let us remember Frank for the things Frank clearly enjoyed.'

The congregation was made to bow their heads in remembrance.

'RIP Frank the Wank.'

47

W A R

The tramp army disappeared from the forty-two rooms around the world to appear on trains, in shopping centres, busy main streets, souks, temples, cinemas, stadiums, airports, train and bus stations, churches, mosques, synagogues, villages, all the places where large numbers gather.

The conversion begins.

Mister Li and the Xaja had felt the disturbance and had been busy with plans to counter the attack. Many Xaja died. Many Tramps died. Many civilians died. All tramps were freed. Some civilians and some Xaja too. It was the end of days. Mayhem, disruption, chaos. The world would not recover.

The Tramps went into battle shouting their war cry

'Spare Some Change, Please?'

Spare some change, please? Consider those words. Could you spare change? Are you willing to change? In that simple act of giving you have changed. In not giving you have also changed. It is the most appropriate war cry. Spare some change?

Once more unto the breach! What the fuck does that mean? Throw yourself to your almost certain death, maybe you'll survive and get a medal for your troubles.

Repeated asking of questions weakens the ego, loosens the grip on you, frees you to be yourself.

Huzzah! - which means kill, Banzai! - ten thousand years, and the Finnish 'Tulta Munille!' - fire at their balls, all too aggressive. Sucking you down into the emotion of anger and courageousness. Battle cries are not necessarily articulate but they all aim to provoke patriotic or religious sentiment. Not the Tramps' war cry. That invokes Freedom, true Freedom.

Dieu et mon droit – 'God and my right' was used to overstate the army's aggressive potential and is still used today. Throw in some bagpipes, drums and horns and you'll have the enemy running. Do a war dance, a Hakka and a bit of taunting and you've won. Shock and awe. Tried and tested. But it doesn't work. If it did there would be no war now. But still the wise rulers repeat the same old tired formulae. And still war comes. The early Roman Empire army marched silently into battle, a fantastic psychological twist. However, the late Roman Empire ruined it all by using '*Nobiscum Deus*' which means 'God With Us', but sounds like 'God's Cock Is Ejaculating'. This explains how the Roman Empire rose and why it fell.

'Spare Some Change, Please!' Now *that* keeps the focus. And the outstretched begging hand represents the taunt, the provocation, nice and subtle. By repeatedly asking questions the ego is weakened, the ego then loosens the grip on you, frees you to be yourself.

Spare Some Change, Please! moves you up into peace and love, both the tramp and the one asked.

Ponder those words. Spare some change please. It does not matter if you give. But *if* you give you should not think about it. You shouldn't give to make yourself feel better or to try to make the recipient's life better. Just give and move on. If you don't give you should also just move on, without thinking, without being outraged, without guilt.

You should not get angry with the person asking. You should not start judging that person, or blaming them for annoying you. You should not assume it's their own wretched fault they are in such a predicament, even though it *is*. You should *not* give and *not* think. Move on. Same principle.

So, those that gave were offered the next choice and those that didn't give were also offered the next choice.

The Christian Crusaders would approach a Moorish Muslim. 'Christianity or death?' Most would say, 'Yeah, OK, I'll take the Christianity, you fucking red-crossed freak, but as soon as your back is turned and as soon as I've got my hands on a scimitar I'll cut you down for being such a prick. In the meantime I'll carry on believing in the words of Allah.' A few would get all moralistic and choose death, rather than betray their mullahs. Fair enough, an equally valid choice.

The correct choice however is to leave the whole thing alone. Transcend the choices. Realise your true nature, and leave the world alone. Be in the world but not of the world. And then you see it for the show it is. The ghost fragment of a tawdry soap opera, compared to the parabrahmic bliss experience you now feel and know. The Divine love that you are.

Violence doesn't work. The sages got that right.

The Tramps had the power to do what I'd done on that train, the power to play the emotion orchestra and create the death-freedom. But they refrained and asked the questions. They still ask the questions now.

'Spare some change?' and then, 'Freedom or death?' And then silence.

Most choose freedom, not understanding what freedom is, but thinking it sounds better than death. It is.

Some choose death, to spite the impertinence of the tramp. This is to be applauded. For to invite death is to know death is not real. And once you know this you have freedom. The questions asked were not just to the mind but also to the spirit. They were allowed to resonate and develop. The silence after the two questions was really the sound of the Aum. The sound of a great crashing ocean, deafeningly glorious to the Tramps, but only subliminally audible to the person being asked. That sound would resonate and build though and eventually the person asked would move, would take steps to free themselves. The Xaja knew this and tried to stop it and in so doing freed the tramps and some civilians and sometimes themselves. I forbade the Tramps to fight the Xaja. They were not to fight anyone. They were simply told to resonate love.

All is well and unfolding exactly as it should.
Eventually all the Tramps will be murdered but by then it will be too late for Mister Li.

All this, of course, was a simple diversion, a misdirection. I had a bigger, much more important task.

That of Mister Li.

48

H O B B I E S

I left the church thanking the sobbing widow. It's good to let the grief out. I patted her on the head. 'That's right love, have a good cry.' I left the envelope containing the photos on the lectern. People would either open the package or not. The rest of the congregation was trying to get to me, but I'm a busy man and my job here was done. A few well-timed suggestions and they were squabbling amongst themselves, desperately looking for someone else to blame for the debacle. I winked at the vicar and he winked back. He knew, he was enlightened in his own way. All those funerals change a man.

The youngsters were suppressing laughter; they still sensed that life is essentially nonsense. That is why children make the best soldiers. That is why children are capable of extraordinarily brutal things. They make the best bullies. They have less fear than adults; they are not fully conditioned to the illusion and completely anchored in the world. This will change when they get the urge to procreate. Wicked thing puberty.

I do love to tell the truth, especially at inappropriate moments. Weddings and funerals, Silver, Gold, Pearl, in fact any wedding anniversary celebration. Christenings are good too. Bar Mitzvahs are strangely more satisfying than Bat Mitzvahs; I suppose the boys are given more freedom than the girls in this backward thinking monstrosity we still have the temerity to call civilization. Funerals are the best, though, no one expects it and I am a sucker for a show. It used to be about wanting approval but now that I am more at peace I realise it is more to ram the fucking point home. Pain is a powerful teacher. You punch a dog on the snout and he thinks twice about biting.

But I don't want your hardcore preaching, Mister Mann, I just want an easier life.

You don't know what you want, you don't know why you are here, you don't have a clue. I'm here to give you one. An enormous one. A big throbbing, veiny, shaft of a clue. If I have to, I will spray that clue all over your face.

In the early days I used to be much cruder, and more into justice than into spreading truth. I would persuade ice-cream van drivers to get back at the brat children by replacing the *Cadbury's* chocolate *Flake* in the 99 cone with a mini chocolate log of their own. When the parents complained, the surprisingly eloquent driver would simply state, 'Kids eh! In our day we used to roll a football in doggy poo and get our mates to head it. Your young Jimmy seems to be a lot more inventive.' And with that simple piece of common nostalgia and the praising of their spoilt child's creativity the driver would be free to pull the same stunt the following week.

Comedians have a very powerful tool. They can spread the truth by making people laugh. There are few comedians that do this well. Most are wrapped up in ego and blame their need to make a living for selling out to advertising and the light entertainment industry. Did Kevin Costner make *A Field of Dreams* for nothing? Build it and they will come. Let go and let God. Use your talent. And be damned. Bill Hicks and Lenny Bruce were comedy sages. They pointed the way. Who do we have today? As far as I can see, just the visionary duo - Breeze & Fabric:

The rest just write material for others to steal.

I wish I was funny.

49

L I

The Tramps were out asking the two questions, and sitting in the silence. The Xaja were out slaughtering the Tramps. Mister Li took his time coming. He expected a fight from the tramp army, your regular eye-for-an-eye, tooth-for-a-tooth reaction, but all he got was love. We were winning everywhere. Mister Li was becoming weak. The public rallied against the initial brutality of the tramp cleansing and Mister Li and the Xaja had to be more subtle in their extermination. Expert hiders, tramps, but eventually they would all be murdered, and be free. Lomas and Gouge had gone into hiding, they might be needed later. Morgan and Varcoe had gone over to the Xaja as planned. They were now sleepers, ready for the contingency plan if my confrontation with Mister Li went awry.

I met him at my place in the City of London, Change Alley. It was a well-hidden room just opposite the *Royal Exchange*; the giant ornamental locusts protruding from the building gave me much comfort. My place was small. Just one room. Thirteen foot by thirteen foot. The only thing hanging from the wall was my insect display cabinet. The only piece of furniture was my *Parker Knoll Ambassador* recliner. One window looked out at the locust statue opposite. The walls were white, pure brilliant white. Not white with a hint of apricot or apple sundae, but white. The walls were electrochromatic and could be changed instantly to black by pressing a button in the arm rest of the recliner. They could in fact display all the colours in the spectrum but I never used that facility. I am not that flippant. The electrochromatic device works like a simple electrolytic cell, when a voltage is applied to some materials under the right conditions they change colour. Chemical chameleons. It's rather like what I do to the human brain. The human displays another nature when my charge is applied; it shows its true colours.

I had tired of my hobbies, my distractions, and had been broadcasting to Mister Li for over a month:

I sent him love. I sent him acceptance. I sent him peace. I invited him to visit.

Come and chat. Let's spend some quality time with each other.

Eventually he came.

I was reclining. He appeared in front of me. A very smooth teleportation. Barely a disturbance. He had learnt well.

'Nice *Parker Knoll*. It's the *Ambassador* isn't it?'

'Yes. Are you a connoisseur?'

'I appreciate perfection when I see it.'

'The wall colour to your liking?' I asked.

'A little stark, you don't happen to have an aquamarine?'

'I'm not a tart.'

'YES YOU ARE.'

'I AM NOT.' The Voice not working on either of us.

'You are. Look what you let Monica do to you the other day.'

'Good point, well presented.'

How does he know these things? No one can read me. No one understands me. No one can read my mind.

'How do you know these things?'

'Haven't you worked it out?'

'Yes.'

'Are you sure?'

'You have spies. Monica blabbed.'

'She's a fucking glove puppet.'

'Spies then.'

'No. No one knows what you think or do. No one can see you.'

'I don't know then. How do you know these things?'

'Because I am you.'

'Don't give me that spiritual nonsense. You know as well as I it is a lie. It doesn't work. It is a tool to herd, marshal, control the masses.'

'No. It is the truth. You are me.'

'I can never be you. You are a monster!'

'Yes I am. I am the Devil, Dispater, Beelzebub, the Horned One. I am the fallen Angel, The Adversary whose job is to test humankind. The trickster, the tempter, Satan, Ha-satan, Shaitan, Abaddon, Lucifer, Belial. I am you. I am Mind. The Mind. The Thinker, The Little Tinker, Iblis, The Dragon, The Cunt Prime, Angra Mainyu, The Lie, Destructive Emanation, The Evil One, Rahu, Kroni, Ravana, Duryodhana, Kaliyan.'

He was good. Pure vaudeville. I'm a sucker for melodrama. That list was exquisite. The pronunciation of those words, faultless. A joy. The perfect baddy. I could do better, though. I stood, I danced as I spoke, pausing in perfect stillness, twirl, and glide, movement so pure.

'OK. I get it. I understand. I get it. You are Mara, The Desires, Devadatta, Set, Apep, Baphomet, Lord of the Flies, Lord of Pride, Despicableness of the Earth, Mastema, Mephisto, He that avoids Light, Sammael Poison of God, 666 or 616 the Number of the Beast, Ahriman, The Antichrist, Malign Spirit, Unholy Spirit, Der Leibhaftige - He Himself, Diabolus, The Downword Flowing, Cuntus Ultima, Lord of this World - I fucking understand, prick. But you are not me, you can never be me!'

'Oh but Mister Mann I am you. You are Old Scratch, The Stranger, Old Nick, Old Hob, Kolski, Voland, Arawn, Baal, Chernobog, Malek Taus, Mammon, Ördög, Pan, Pazuzu, Pwcca, Supay, Typhon, Vritra, The Prince of Darkness, The Source of All Evil, A Demon, A Tyrant. You are Cunt.'

'You are not me. You are not me. You are not me.'

'Mister I am you. Mann I am you. Mister Mann - I am you.'

Silence.

'Send me love, Mister Mann or I'll go away and we'll battle again. I can feel your hate rising. Run away again, little man. This is your chance. You have helped so many others. Why not help yourself? You have died over a million times; you have felt every one of those deaths. Why die anymore? They are not your children, let them go. Die no more and live.'

'No.'

'Have you ever killed anyone?'

'No.'

'That is right, you haven't. You have merely persuaded them to see the truth and allowed them to take responsibility for their actions. You really are the Light Bringer. You really are Lucifer. True, you instigated the thought processes that led to their actions, but ultimately they all took their own lives or the lives of others, they were responsible for their own actions, they did nothing that was not already within them. Just like government does, you provided the suggestions, it was up to the people to follow those orders or not. You were the general, the politician, the king, but ultimately the people were accountable. As your

Tramp Army are so eloquently phrasing it now 'Freedom or Death?' We are all going to die, and we are all free right now, but few appreciate that.'

'I am not you.'

'Tut, tut, send me love or I disappear. AND WE FIGHT AGAIN.'

Tricky feller, this one. I really do like to fight. I really do like a good show down, a good list to recite with melodrama, invoke a show. He was playing me well. He was playing me really well. Only I could play myself that well. Very persuasive, a true master, he had grown strong with me. The Deceiver, The Tempter.

'Do you know what you must do?'

'No. It is done. I have won. You are defeated. XAJA is defeated. It will take time, but it will work.'

'Don't be ridiculous. You have merely stalled. Clever, you have reversed the cycle but the ebb and flow continues. We will evolve. We will become more inventive and eventually the good you have done will be used against the world and even more cruel and horrendous tortures will take place. I shall ask you again:

Do you know what you must do?

That was new.

Different evolution of the Voice? No compulsion, no coercion. Just an overwhelming willingness to embrace a fact. To dig deep and see - FINALLY. I understood.

'I must kill you.'

'Yes, my dear, you must. Step off the ledge, trust. Kill me. Feel the Loning? Embrace it. The unknown. No one has been here. Leave everything behind. By perceiving the reality you gain dominion. Those who are possessed by nothing possess everything. I am you. Kill me.'

'But you don't exist.'

'Neither do you. Kill me.'

'But it was all for nothing?'

'Yes. It is all meaningless. Kill me!'

'No, I can't do that. You are me.'

'Then kill me! Do it! Kill me!'

'No!'

'Then we fight some more. We fight again. And again. Kill me. Or I will suppress your freedom, your kindness, your love. I will mutilate your peace. I will drive you to the ledge and make you jump. I will visit you and urinate on your twisted form, again and again and again. I will not stop. Over and over. And your mother shall weep as your pathetic frame desperately clings to what weak life you have left. I will crush you until you snap! Kill me now!'

I leapt, I twisted, the neck snapped. My straight tensed fingers punched a hole in the right side of his chest and pulled out his black heart. I did it all with love.

I sat back in the recliner and looked out of the window at the locust opposite.

I opened my eyes for the first time in thirty-three years and looked at the room.

50

K A R M A

The word karma means action. The law of karma is taught in every religion and culture in the world. It is not just the preserve of tofu-eating, self-obsessed middle class hypocrites.

In the Bible it is stated 'As you sow, so shall you reap'. In the *Tibetan Book of the Dead* it is phrased, 'Gunga galunga... gunga, gungala gunga'. In the farming community: 'If you plant cabbages, you can't expect to harvest tomatoes.'

Every thought, every word, every deed in our lives is a seed which we plant in the world. We harvest the fruits of those seeds. Anger, fear, desire and doubt. Love, kindness and understanding. Which seeds do you choose to sow? Don't answer that question. Because it doesn't matter.

This is not philosophy, it is a simple law. What goes around comes around. A law of energy. Karma is sometimes immediate; you flick a switch the light goes on, you step on a rake, it smacks you in the face. Often karma is delayed; you set an alarm clock and ten hours later it goes off and frightens you. A kindness that we think went unnoticed; something terrible that we hoped would disappear. Nothing ever falls through the cracks. It is coming to get you. When you understand karma you have a choice, carry on hurting people or practise Ahimsa - no harm to any person, animal or thing.

No two people have the same karma, but the journey of 'working it all out' is basically the same. As we become more aware of the process we tend to cooperate more and more. That is why I cooperated with the Devil. He asked me to kill him so I did. But not with hate, with love. My action seemed brutal but I had nothing but love in my heart as I looked at his still beating in my hand.

All beings are connected. This One-ness is the Truth, real and natural. Any thought, word or deed which creates a feeling of separateness creates more karma; it creates the illusion of falseness. Working out karma is simply undoing this falseness in order to return to the Truth, the Oneness.

This is why Mahatma Gandhi said to his assassin, 'I'm sorry, my son.' He believed in and understood karma. He didn't want to have another round. This is why Jesus said on the cross, 'Forgive them Father, for they know not what they do.' People who understand karma simply don't hurt other people. They don't want it coming back again and again. These sages had done their homework. They realised they were absolute cunts in the past and enough was enough, they would take whatever was coming to them and not complain.

We are all connected.

51

L O C U S T

Alocust is a type of grasshopper that changes colour and behaviour when it gets crowded by other locusts. Humans, in their way, do the same. Increased tactile stimulation of the grasshopper's hind legs causes its levels of serotonin to rise. Serotonin, the happy chemical. You see how we are all connected? We humans produce and are affected by serotonin. It keeps us calm, makes us sleep better and relieves depression. In a locust this drug causes colour change, encourages voracious eating and the urge to breed more freely. Same with humans. Stimulation of the legs, at a rate of thirty times a minute over a four hour period, triggers locusts to swarm. In humans it takes a little longer. The largest locust swarm covered hundreds of square miles and contained a billion highly-coordinated insects. The largest human swarm covers the whole earth and contains seven billion barely coordinated creatures.

The locust I was staring at was The Gresham Grasshopper. Sir Thomas Gresham founded the *Royal Exchange* in 1565; his grasshoppers adorn the walls of that magnificent building. The founder of the family, Roger de Gresham, was abandoned as a newborn in long grass in North Norfolk in the 13th Century. A passing woman's attention was drawn to the baby by the unusually loud noise of a grasshopper. The grasshopper saved that life.

Male grasshoppers have bollocks that produce spunk. The female gets shagged by the male, doggy style, and her eggs are fertilised by his ejaculate. Remarkably like the average human sex life. Grasshoppers spend nine months in the egg; humans spend nine months in the womb. A hatched grasshopper lives for three months. Humans should learn from this.

That grasshopper saved his life.

I stared at the statue. Sub order *Caelifera* in the order *Orthopetra*. I noticed I had a grasshopper in my insect cabinet. Why? There were loads of the perishers where I grew up.

The grasshopper on the side of the building I could see through my window was female. Short antennae, tympana on the side of the first abdominal segment. Long strong hind femora. She was a large one, beautiful, golden. The tegmina were not fit for flight not for the usual reason of being coriaceous but because they were made of metal. Two pairs of valves at the end of her abdomen. I imagined the inside of her biology. The stomodaeum, the proctodaeum and the mesenteron. The muscular pharynx leading to the malpighian tubules. I considered the ileum and rectum. My mind ranged to the nervous system, to the controlling ganglia in each of the sections including the head, acting as a brain. The central neuropile reacting to the sense external organs manifesting as sensilla. The most dense congregation of sensilla on the antennae, palps, cerci and tympanal organs. All linked to the neuropile and then to the brain. Exquisite detail in one so small. So human. I decided to get intimate, she wouldn't mind. She was a statue, made of metal, cold, uncaring. But she seemed warmer now. More accessible. Because of my attention. My longing to discover her. She seemed larger too. Not a small insect any more, not a large six foot statue either. Larger, warmer, more approachable. I imagined her sex organs, her ovipositor - never to experience the joy of an aedeagus depositing a spermatophore. The fine micropyles, receiving life from the haemolymph.

As I pondered she moved. She opened her wings. I had excited her? The accessory pumps started and flushed the wing veins with green blood. I had aroused her? The legs and antennae charged too, the circulation completed by returning to the abdomen. She twitched. Wings unfolded. Legs flexed. The green viscous blood continued to pump and fill the body cavities and appendages. The heart and aorta increased their efforts until, finally, the whole glorious system vibrated with life. She breathed, tracheae, air-filled tubes, pairs of spiracles. Tracheoles carrying oxygen. Her salivary glands secreted digestive enzymes. Protease, lipase, amylase oozed.

She looked at me. She was fully cognisant. Her wings flexed, her legs tensed. She leapt, flew and crashed through the window and into my room.

She sat opposite me in a strange half-human, half-insect pose; resting on the abdominal tail, legs squat, torso erect. Her antennae swept back and disappeared. The other appendages formed arms, which lay crossed. She looked shocked. Disbelieving. Unsure. Her mouth opened. She spoke. I understood.

'My God!'

I realised.

'Mother?'

'Yes, Yes! My God!'

Oh dear. I hadn't seen my mum for thirty-three years and the thing that brought her to life was me thinking about her vagina.

GERRARD G. GERRARD

52

P R E O R D A I N E D

I asked you which seeds of thought you choose to sow, I will tell you how you answered. If you are a coward you will claim you try your best to think good thoughts. You'll say, 'In general my thoughts are good. Come judgement day, on balance, my thoughts will hold me up and show me to be, by and large, good and deserving of a reward. This is ninety-nine point nine nine nine nine percent (99.9999%) of the population.

If you are brave you will have come to the realisation you are an utter cunt and your thoughts are nasty, evil and completely self-serving. This is zero point zero zero zero zero nine nine three three four percent (0.000099334%) of the population. Well done.

If you are wise you will say, 'It doesn't matter what I think, Mister Mann, as everything is preordained and unfolding exactly as it should.' This is zero point zero zero zero zero zero zero six six six percent (0.000000666%) of the population. Go to the top of the class.

You go through the vicissitudes of life and your dogmatic thinking begins to drop away and your heart opens. You begin to feel something different. You begin to loosen up. The first thing you realise is that everything that has transpired in your life has been absolutely necessary. The second thing you realise is that everything has been preordained; everything was supposed to happen the way it happened. There are no mistakes. Now go a step further. Try to understand the third step, understand that the first two steps are a pack of lies, a complete fabrication, for they do not exist in reality.

Everything is preordained only if you believe you are a body and a mind. Everything is karmic, only if you believe you are a body and mind, as long as you identify with the world and believe you are the doer.

It is time to wake up.

You are such an ego. The truth is that your body is an automaton. Your mind is a fool riding around in the automatic body. The body has been programmed to do what it does. Every last detail has been taken care of. What sex you are. How you age. What diseases you receive, the colour of your hair, the tanning ability of your skin, the ideas that you think you have. Everything. Nothing is left to chance. You as a mind-body have no free will. It does not exist for this mechanism. Everything is being taken care of. The accidents you have, the people you fall in and out of love with, the hate, the moments of anger, the years of rage.

Everything.

Don't you see? Your mind is a fool riding on this program, this fairground ride. Your job is to wake up and realise this. The mind, *your* mind, is not your friend. It is a deceiver. It is a fool. It thinks it is in charge, it is not. The body makes a cup of tea, the mind thinks it's doing it. It isn't. The body gets up in the morning, brushes its teeth, showers, shits, wanks, and then has breakfast. The mind thinks it has made all those decisions. It hasn't. Preordained. Everything. Wake up. You can feel it, beneath the mind, which is now frantically telling you not to believe this.

Put down the book it is dangerous.

Go and have a nice cup of tea.

Skip this bit and go to the bits with the designer violence and outrageous statements.

This is dangerous to me and you.

Me and you? How can there be two of you in there? That doesn't make sense. It's just me, the mind. Or is it something else?

He's getting boring and not very clear with his argument, throw this book away, it's rubbish.

But you read on. Because there is something in this.

Here goes:

You have an idea for an original story or joke and you tell this to someone. Sometimes, quite often actually, they will look at you blankly as if they don't understand. You will feel slightly foolish. But you will remember this incident. That is good because it is a clue to a much larger story. A week later the person you told the idea to approaches you and says, 'I've been thinking. What if everything was preordained. What if my body was a robot and my mind a fool, a fool that thinks it is in charge but isn't? The body is pre-programmed to do everything; from making a cup of tea to coming up with the cure for cancer. But my mind is so arrogant it thinks it has created and made all the decision for its life. Wouldn't that make sense?'

And you look at this person in disbelief, because they have just repeated *almost* word-for-word what you said to them a week before. This happens often in life. Look for it. Challenge it. It's not plagiarism. It is a shadow of the much larger program running. All the minds jumping on events, thoughts and ideas and trying to make them their own. The mind trying to justify its existence.

Can you see? Are you getting some of this? It is important. Because the reality is that nothing is original. It has all been done before. And will be done again. Over and over again. For millennia. Until you wake up. Until you transcend the mechanism. Wake up. Work on yourself.

And so I woke up.

53

R O O M

A boy, ten years old, born into a poor dysfunctional broken family.

His character was peace. His true nature - Love. He didn't fit in. He wouldn't fight.

He was driven to contemplate his existence on a window ledge one hundred and fifty-six inches above the ground. He would return to that ledge daily and look, consider, stare at the ground below. Soon the ground became his only friend. The more he stared the closer it got. At first it seemed so far away. But after a long intimate relationship of years they merged. Broken skull, blood and twisted flesh with cold red and black tiles. The head-first impact wasn't enough to kill. It was just enough to paralyse the body and shock the brain into another world. A world where he survived the test with body and mind intact. All the while his original body remained twisted but loved by his mother. Perception is reality.

That boy woke up thirty-three years later.

I looked around the room. The *Parker Knoll* recliner was the same, the *Ambassador Deluxe* 1984 special edition, *still* in my opinion the finest piece of upholstered elegance money can buy. The simplicity of the manual recline, the choice of durable yet luxurious nylon cloth, the elegant robust lines and contours of a masterpiece. 1984 must have been the year I was allowed to go home from the hospital. Eight years of hospital care, must have been serious. The voices came:

spinal
severe
severed
punctured
lung
iron
lung
neck
fracture
neck
weak
twisted
pain
what
relief
killers
pain
killers
broken
shattered
internal
bleeding
impact
problem
reluctance
wake
up
reluctance... to... wake... up

I looked at the wall.

The white starkness of the electrochromatic cell was gone and old wallpaper was in its place. The cabinet was there, the insect collection, but it was cruder and more child-like in creation. The dates had changed too, ranging only over a four year period, from 1972 to 1976. The labels had been tampered with. The weapon used was a later addition. Scrawled on with biro. Underneath that was the place of the find.

Ant - Formicidae - 1972 - The Patio - Old age (Kettle)
Wasp - Vespidae - 1972 - Window - Old age (Daily Mail)
Bee - Andrenidae - 1973 - Flower bed - Old age (Lethal injection)
Fly - Brachycera - 1973 - Sandwich - Old spider web (Sandwiched)
Dragonfly - Aeshnidae - 1974 - Pond - Floating (Drowning)
Moth - Drepanidae - 1974 - Wardrobe - Old age (Dry cleaning plastic)
Earwig - Forficulidae - 1975 - Park - Old age (Andy's face)
Butterfly - Nymphalidae - 1975 - Garden - On lawn (Secateurs)
Grasshopper - Acrididae - 1976 - Outside - Front drive (Strangled)
Beetle - Noteridae - 1976 - Patio - Under log (Magnifying glass)

The inscription was different too. More simplistic. Instead of 'Something in the insect seems to be alien to the habits, morals, and psychology of this world, as if it had come from some other planet: more monstrous, more energetic, more insensate, more atrocious, more infernal than our own.' was 'Beauty is only skin deep.' - *Mum - 1974*

This young boy was so tender that he refused to kill the insects he collected. All were dried old insects found in nature already deceased. Even the fly was taken from an old disused web because the child knew that spiders had to survive and by taking the fly from a living web he would be depriving the arachnid of its hard earned food. Who was he to judge their nature? A sensitive, tortured youth who was continually bullied because he refused to join in with the herd, the common gang, refused to judge, criticise, persecute and victimise outsiders. A child who decided to try to take his life rather than join in with the world. What do you know of dreams? Simple pleasures? What do you know of dreams or reality?

I surveyed the rest of the cluttered room. Everywhere books piled high. And videos, an old television where the window used to be. Postcards decorated the walls. Hundreds of them. Who were they from? Who were they for? I wanted to know - I knew, but I wanted to know for sure. No mirrors. And the window was covered with a very old, dusty net curtain, once white but now grey. The fibres were black with dirt and dust but what little light it let through gave the illusion that it was grey.

The titles I could make out on the spine of the books, showed *The Bible*, *The Koran*, *The Torah*, *The Vadas*, practically every major religious treatise, there was even something by David Ike. Someone had been searching for answers. She had read them all to me. Encyclopaedias, Professor Hawking, Carl Sagan, Arthur C. Clarke, Frank Herbert, Tolkien (happily no J.K. Rowling) Phillip K. Dick, Terry Southern, Jim Thompson, Hayek, physics books on everything from Chaos to String Theory, Trachtenberg System, Wu Cheng, Morihei Ueshiba, Erdnase, Shakespeare, Chaucer, Dicky Feynman, books on Trading, Neural Networks, Artificial Intelligence, Finance, Economics, Asimov, Berkoff, Roy Walton, Bobo, Huggard and Braue, Banachek, Luke Jermay, Alfred Tack, Harry Lorayne, dictionaries, a thesaurus, Elizabeth Wurtzel (what a fox), Trudi Canavan, Virginia Woolf, Richard Dawkins, the latter no doubt in a desperate attempt to enrage me from my coma, the fabulous Douglas

Adams, a friend of Dawkins - what a true saint that man was, he loved everyone. Darwin, Kahlil Gibran, Homer, Ambrose Bierce, Peter and Craig Wilson, Steinbeck, Bob Monkhouse, Damásio, Geoffrey Household, Easton Ellis (explaining my fascination for lists), Peter Cook, Anne Rice, Bram Stoker, travel books, gardening books, books on insects and biology, moths and butterflies, Roald Dahl, Milligan, Chris and Simon Donald, Graham Dury, Simon Thorp, Edward Gorey, Sendak, Beatrix Potter, Enid Blyton and Gurdjieff. Those were just some that I could make out. The video collection was equally extensive, ranging from the BBC's *Life on Earth* to *It's a Wonderful Life*. The music collection from *Great Medical Disaster* to *Red Star Line*.

All that information had been subliminally pumped into me over thirty-three years, in a barbaric attempt to wake me up.

I didn't stand a chance.

My mother, desperate to save her baby. She must not fail; it became her mission, her reason to be. It became her obsession, her life.

What had I done to her? What misery had I caused? I felt shame. For the first time in thirty-three years I felt heavy, suffocating shame, humiliation, a deep unfathomable regret. I had tortured this poor woman with my selfishness, with that decision.

What had she done to deserve this?

Thirty-three years tending a cripple, a toxic waste-producing, twisted wreck of a being who'd once been her beautiful kind, caring and loving son. Freedom or death, indeed.

I looked at my body. It was weak. Atrophied muscles ache, sore pressure points.

I could blink. Facial muscles could work slowly.

Speech?

'Mmmmthrrrrr?'

Nope, not yet. She understood though.

Silly cow. Should have left me to die.

She will be the first to kill herself when I'm strong enough.

'Is that you, Mister Mann?'

'Wahoo Mohammed! Yep.'

54

C O M A

A coma is a profound state of unconsciousness. *Locked-in Syndrome* is where a patient is aware and awake, but cannot move or communicate due to complete paralysis of all voluntary muscles. It is like being buried alive. What happened to me was not a coma and not *Locked-in Syndrome*. But people like to label and diagnose. I was diagnosed as comatose. They thought I didn't respond to pain, they thought I couldn't hear, they thought I had regressed to a vegetative state. I had no normal awareness of the outside world, their outside world. But my world was very real. I felt pain, I laughed, cried, I had emotions, I thought, I acted. I was alive. I simply refused to wake up. I had resolved into another reality.

Comas can last anything from two days to forty years. My thirty-three years was extremely rare but not unique. What was unique was my recovery. Recovering from a coma usually occurs gradually. Some patients never progress beyond very basic responses, but many make complete recoveries. The outcome of a coma and vegetative state depends on the cause, location, severity and extent of neurological damage. The length of time or deepness of coma does not matter. I emerged from my 'coma' with physical, intellectual and deep psychological problems. Not the usual physical problems associated with recovering patients. Not the usual intellectual problems, and certainly not the usual psychological problems.

Doctors love to diagnose. They tell you what you've got but very rarely cure you. In fact you always cure yourself; it is your body doing the curing. The doc just gives you some pills, usually placebo but they can't admit that because their businesses would fail. If they do give you some 'medicine' it's usually a synthetic derivative of something that can be found in nature for free. Does the medicine really cure? Is there such a thing as a germ? Has the doctor ever seen one? Ask him. Watch him squirm. Hear him talk about microscopic imaging. Act like a child and drill down.

But how do you know that's a germ? How does the technique of imagining work? Does it destroy what is there and leave a shadow? Is it the actual germ? What is light? What is energy? Is a germ energy?

Keep it up and eventually he will cave in. Anything to get you out of his surgery.

Disease, illness, germs, virus, bacteria - all mind stuff. Leave it alone and be well.

'You've got Winklebrat's Disease.'

'Oh yes, Dr Winklebrat and what exactly is that?'

'The symptoms you are displaying, and a few more that I'll jot down in my notes just to make sure, to catch a few outliers. Perhaps you could think about the other symptoms and catch them too. That would be great.'

'Have you just made up Winklebrat's Disease, doctor?'

'Yes. That will be a large sum of money and worldwide recognition for me please, and a long, drawn-out death for you if you fall for it.'

Crooks, the lot of them. They should go back to grave robbing.

55

C R I P P L E

That is it. That is my destiny. To be a cripple. Not like the raspberries you know, the famous ones. The brave Para Olympians or the usefully brainy Stevie Hawking types. No, I am the selfish self-obsessed type. Crippled not only in body but also in mind. Twisted, broken, damaged beyond repair. Disgusting.

Just because I'm a cripple it doesn't mean I'm nice. It doesn't mean I am brave, it doesn't mean I am loving. I had learnt to love implicitly in the other world. And now I must learn to do it all again. And the doctors called this progress. It certainly means I am angry, such rage you could not imagine. It means that I have desires. It means I have lust. I want to walk, I want to embrace someone, anyone. Even Monica? If she would have me. I want to control, I want to have approval, I want security. I want. I want. I want. And it means that I fear. I am the biggest idiot you will ever meet. How do you think I became a cripple? Yep, by being an idiot.

'Oh look, a cripple. Ah bless, brave little soldier. Must be hard. So it's OK if you want to be a complete twat, you have a lot to contend with.'

Wrong thinking. Next time I run over your foot in my wheelchair pretending it was an accident, but actually hating you because you can walk, call me a cunt and move on. Better still, tip me out of the chair, slash the tyres and give my chariot a thorough keying for good measure. Kick me, call me a cunt and then move on. But how do you know if it wasn't an accident? Just do it, I deserve it. I deserve worse. But that will come later.

'Tut tut, Mister Mann. Is that self pity?'

'Yes, Mister Mann, I think it is.'

'You know better than that. Perceive reality and gain dominion.'

I eventually tired of playing the cripple card and of wallowing in self pity and decided to get better. I'd come this far. I had learnt from the other world that it was possible to create things. Small things at first. I had awakened myself from the coma, from the very powerful illusion that was my reality. It was time to wake up again. From the illusion of the body. Small steps. Mister Mann was there to help me. To encourage me. We would remember the good times. The times when we had ultimate power.

'Keep going, little one, perceive reality and gain dominion. Send your body love. Heal. Get better. Release the negativity. It is not your fault. The guilt is not yours, all preordained, everything is unfolding exactly as it should. All is well. We will be back on our feet in no time. Keep going. Send the love. More love. Love infinite. Love divine. I am so proud of you. No regrets. Victory for freedom. Keep going.'

I didn't regain the power of speech for a long time. But I could move my eyelids. I could type short messages with a rapidly healing finger. Those hands - such power.

I could communicate with the new world. One of the first messages I typed was this:

```
Mum. He has pissed on me again. He has been
doing it for years. When you were in the
kitchen making him a cup of tea. No, Mum, I'm
not joking. The times I shat myself? It
wasn't because I was pleased to see him. It
was because he was smearing me with his own
faeces. Don't leave me in a room alone with
him again, Mum. He hates me, Mum. He always
has.
```

Took me four hours to pen that beauty. I exaggerated about the excrement, but the rest was true.

The visits from my brother stopped shortly after that. Apparently he didn't appreciate my humour. I don't know where he is. Those postcards will tell me. Those mocking cards.

I can move, I can travel. You are a cripple.

He would always visit after a long plane journey. Terrible brown, rancid piss, dehydrated by a twenty-four hour flight from the other side of the world. I'm glad it has stopped.

That is what I call progress, doctors.

56

G O D

I suppose I have always been Mister Mann. Not the gentle child. Not the kind, loving, peaceful boy. Mister Mann is also the gentle child, he is everything.

As soon as I could stand again I became Mister Mann. The child was there, but buried deep. Locked away to play forever with his beautiful insects. At peace, in joy and forever loving.

But Mister Mann's love is more evolved.

And she lay there.

She had been dead thirty minutes now. I looked at her carcass. I had the power to resurrect her but she had suffered enough. She had cared for me no matter what. Sacrificed her life for mine. I love her so much. A hard, terrible life and she deserved to die. She deserved the release.

And so you judge me. I am you.

Before the last breath left her lungs I whispered a soothing message:

'Whatever you believe is wrong with your life or with the world is nothing but an unfoldment in consciousness. It is necessary for your evolution. If you understand this you will not react to whatever happens. You will not react to me choking the life from you. You will simply smile. There is nothing in the universe that can hurt you. I cannot hurt you. The universe is divine love, pure consciousness. It does not know the meaning of evil or sin. Those are words humans made up. Identify with your true nature as you feel your windpipe crush. Your true nature is love, as is mine. So sail through this so called calamity of your son strangling you. Don't identify with the world or you will suffer. You'll become angry and upset, and disillusioned because this isn't turning out the way you expected. Things are not unfolding the way you think they should according to your preconceived ideas and concepts. There is nothing wrong. Your body is dying. Everything is right the way it is. As you begin to understand this you will find peace. I love you, Mum.'

I looked at her form. The silence was perfect. I could feel her peace. Then I noticed the slight twitch in her cheek. The old wrinkles moving, quivering. Then the eyelid flutter. She was still alive. Why wouldn't she die? God. Anger. Why?

'Woman! You've ruined this moment, this exquisite moment. Was that speech for nothing? Ruined! You selfish, unfeeling cow. Why can't you leave me alone?'

And I began kicking. I kicked and kicked and screamed 'DIE!' The rage consumed me, overwhelmed me. She turned her face toward me. Eyes staring in disbelief. Those eyes. I kicked that face. And kicked. I kicked until the eyes turned red and stared no more. Screaming. '*Leave me alone. Die! Woman. Mother. Leave me to myself. Stop interfering. Leave me alone.*'

And I kicked with all my might. Exhaustion started to come. But still I kicked.

'We give it intellectual understanding but IT is not understandable. Experience is the key. You want ANSWERS! I can explain for an infinity what an orange feels and tastes like in your mouth but you will still not understand. The best way is for you to eat it! Why won't you die?'

She was now finally dead but I was so alive. I continued kicking and preaching.

'You must want this freedom more than anything else. More than relationships, more than possessions, more than a mother, a father, a wife, a child. More than a son!'

I stopped.

I looked.

What had I done?

I foetused.

Rocking. Foetus. Sob. Foetus.

Guilty little foetus.

Despised foetus.

Terrible foetus.

Parasite foetus clinging to the womb wall.

Disgusting foetus.

Foetus

Ovum

Sperm

Thought

Space

Nothing

No thing

Then Her voice came.

'To err is human, to forgive is Divine.'

I forgave myself.

I stood up and became God.

57

D I A M O N D

I see you all, every one of you lovely human beings, like beautiful shining, sparkling diamonds covered in shit. Some of you are more covered than others, but you are all diamonds underneath. Some of you are covered in that white crusty, dry stuff we used to call poodle poo when we were young. Odourless, crumbly, easy to get off your shoe when you step in it. But most are covered in the rancid, sticky, vile smelling excrement that comes from the arse of a leper that has a curried doner kebab fetish.

You all move around pretending to puppet your automaton bodies, the carcasses of flesh and bone, toxic waste-producing vehicles that you beguile yourself into combing, polishing, washing and caring for. Intoxicating, drugging yourselves with entertainment, food, drink and drugs and sex with other shit-covered carcasses. Refusing to look at the diamond you are. Wonderfully ridiculous, brilliantly, infinitely perverted. Occasionally a hero is presented to you, a Jesus, a Buddha, or the other one, a sage, someone who pushes the envelope of deadness, wakes you up and urges you to reflect on your existence. They nudge you to freedom, and you feel better. You get comfortable and stop and around and around you go.

And you say, 'Mister Mann, I understand intellectually that if the world is defined by the mind's perception then it has no foundation in reality, because thoughts are not real. They do not exist and so the world cannot exist. And therefore I don't exist either. In your definition of existence there is nothing that exists because there is nothing that is tangible, because perception defines tangibility, and perception is simply a thought, and thoughts are not tangible because they do not exist. But Mister Mann, the suggestion made by this, that thought and perception are one and the same is true on a biological level. Chemical and electrical signals in the brain and body work to affect thought and perception in a similar manner. But is it correct to assume that sensory perception and thought are no different? It seems to me that your definition of existence is too narrow. When I hear the word 'exist' I assume it is referring to something that 'is', or rather something that 'is not a lack of something'. Making nothing the subject of a sentence makes it into something, and therefore a paradox. I understand 'what is' and 'what is not' depends solely on my perception.

But it is not true to say that nothing exists without my perception of it. Nothing exists for me maybe, but it still may be there when my perception is taken away. So is there nothing without the mind's perception? Is it possible that the only way to understand non-existence is that non-existence is that which the mind cannot fathom or perceive, and by that definition it is impossible to ever reach a higher state of awareness? And if that were true, might it also be true that enlightenment is just another state of mind?'

And I say, 'I'm not a fucking philosopher.'

It is all mind stuff. Switch off the mind and feel it. If you insist I'll join in with your word wanking. But just for a bit, because I refuse to cum forever. It is a massive waste of energy.

Mister Mann unzips and gets out his concept cock and gently strokes its mighty length and girth.

Thought is like a mass that distorts awareness, grabs hold of it and creates a condition, such as an apparent object.

Without thought to give the formless awareness form, there would be no form, no object, no external world.

The hypothesis twitches and grows with engorgement.

When you no longer identify with your thoughts, they lose the ability to create forms, including objects. Then they are seen to be unreal. Shadows or ghosts compared to the 'seer', who is you. You have the primary existence, all else is secondary to you, impermanent, having no substance. You as a person are nothing in this scheme, just an imaginary passing form.

The shiny bulb of deduction glistens in the half light of realisation.

Ultimately awareness, the *real*, or whatever you call it, cannot be described or defined. You need to go beyond this bottleneck of trying to understand with words.

The rhythm of postulation quickens, the pre-cum of presupposition rises.

The mind will never give you freedom. Wake up, smell the amyl nitrate, taste the orange, feel the cream. Practise; stop the discussing and start being.

There is no birth or death or karma for one who has realised the knowledge 'I AM'. He has gone beyond it, transcended it.

The groan of axioms, the moan of thesis, the cum-cry of inference.

This is something very important to understand. Just the verbal understanding of the knowledge 'I AM' is altogether different from actual realisation. There are many who will verbally or theoretically understand the 'I AM', yet only the rarest of the rare will realise it. Why? Because realising means transcending it, and you no longer are an individual, you are unborn, there is no question of death. It is the end of it all!

Pull out Mister Mann!

Conjectural conclusion cum all over your derivatively deductive dignity.

58

T E A

You have judged me.
You have changed.
That is as it is.

I stood and contemplated what had just happened. I was fully recovered now. The rehabilitation had been surprisingly quick. The doctors were amazed. Just under a year from the emergence of the coma to healthy, fit, toned, tight-bunned, buff forty-three year-old. I looked, felt, and was good.

But those episodes would come. Seething rages. Delusions they said. Psychological echoes, shadows that would fade with time. Something to do with trauma. Something to do with programs.

What did they know?

They were so real. So positively real.

I had killed her.

Killed the one who was always there, who gave unconditional love, who taught me to love.

They say you hurt the ones you love the most, don't they?

She handed me a cup of tea and a generous slice of angel cake.

'Did it just happen again?

'Yes.'

'Still as real?'

'Yes.'

'Anything different this time?'

'Yes. I forgave myself.'

'That's good.'

'Mum, I'm scared.'

She held me tight. She knew words were useless. We sat in the silent embrace.

We sat in the silence.

'Whatever happens, Mum, just know, whatever I do, whatever happens, I will always love you.'

She held me tighter and whispered, 'I would die a thousand times or more for you.'

59

B R O T H E R

Aｎd so you judged, and so you changed.

There was a mother who had two sons. They grew up and went out into the world. One became a successful businessman, employed many people, provided jobs and security for many. The other developed himself, took vows of silence, entered into spiritual teachings, studied the ancient texts, learnt many powers and secrets, powers of levitation, water into wine, raising the dead, healing the lame, curing the blind, fish and loaves into more fish and loaves - all the classics.

One day the mother asked her sons what they had achieved.

The first son said I have businesses providing work, food, shelter and prosperity for many people. She was pleased. She asked the second son what he had achieved.

He said, 'Come with me, Mother.' He took her down to the river and began to recite ancient words of power, evoke spirits and after much ceremony he walked on top of the water and crossed the river.

She said, 'Bloody fool, there's a bridge just there. Why didn't you use that?'

I approached his offices. Would I use my powers or just the gun?

'I am his brother, come to see my brother.'

Mister Mann had gone now but he had left me gifts.

And he had left me with a choice. Revenge and another trip on the karmic merry-go-round.

'I am my brother, come to see his brother.'

or…

'I am my brother, my brother is me.'

Freedom.

'We are everything. We became Cain, we became Abel. We are everything and we are no thing.'

He set me free. He made me realise.

I know what you are thinking.

I know how you change.

I know how you judge.

I know you.

I love you.

I love.

I.

I…

I AM.

I AM MAN.

T H E   E N D

APPENDIX

PARABRAHMANN

'There is nothing either good or bad,
but thinking makes it so.'
- William Shakespeare

www.parabrahmanmeup.blogspot.com

Mahatma Andy has stopped blogging. He has found peace. His blog is recorded here as he would have wanted:

Mahatma Andy
London, United Kingdom
I discovered a short while ago that Mahatma was Sanskrit for 'Great Soul'. I always thought it was Indian for Keith.

MONDAY, 6 OCTOBER 2008
HAPPINESS

I've been having increasingly regular glimpses into: freedom/awareness/parabrahmen/choiceless/effortless/perfection/happiness/the thing without description, so I thought I'd write down how I got to these states. Useful reminder for me and it might be useful to some seekers to have a raw account of ego elimination too. I'll detail the events as they happened, conditions, preparation and all that. What was the school thing? Method/Results/Conclusion?

TUESDAY, 7 OCTOBER 2008
SURROUND YOURSELF WITH FEAR

I've had many peak experiences in my life. We all have, but we forget to remember. Beautiful view, birth of my children, getting caught in and surviving a bomb blast. But they have all been short-lived. Mind takes over and I start thinking again.

I was staring into a friend's eyes listening to his fear – five kids, credit crunch, huge mortgage, passed over for promotion all these years and now going to lose his job, reputation in tatters. I do that all the time. Beat myself up and don't look at what is real.

Can I remain positive despite what is happening around me?

I was due to meet up with another set of friends but I could feel the onset of another peak experience, and whilst I love them dearly… what would you choose? Another set of fear stories or potential bliss? I meditated on the train, then picked up Eckhart Tolle's *The Power of Now*. This is a book I have been resisting for some time. I know why now. My ego hates it. It was recommended to me by one of my gurus. I have many gurus – bizarrely, mostly Scottish. I also have many rugus. This is a term I use for people who annoy me intensely. Gu - dark, Ru - light. So my gurus take me from the dark and lead me to the light. My rugus take me from the light and lead me to the dark. I love gurus and rugus equally. They are both excellent teachers.

My most powerful rugu is my ego. Great teacher, fabulous task master, evil little rascal. I call him Keith. He is also my most powerful guru.

One of my Scottish gurus - Goddess McBeautiful - recommended *The Power of Now* several years ago. I ignored her, knew better - anything that popular can't be good, etc. I read the sentence 'It is not uncommon for people to spend their whole life waiting to start living.' Which brought to mind a host of similar quotes culminating in the Zen - 'If not now, when?' And then I realised I had all this head knowledge and just wasn't doing it. Then another one of my Scottish gurus - McGod - popped into my head and reminded me of something he had said the day before: 'Don't read about it, do it.' Ping! I woke up.

Words can't describe the experience. They can hint at it. Awaken something in the reader/listener - and then that person should follow that personal path. The more words you use, the farther away from it you become. I texted McGod: 'Hahaha! I've just woken up! Mate, it is now!' The experience lasted into the night and most of the next morning. I sat up marvelling at everything, simple stuff was the best. It's not for everyone. You have to be utterly fearless. Most people surround themselves in fear. You have to give that up. Very difficult - until you do it.

'When an opponent comes forward, move in and greet him; if he wants to pull back, send him on his way.'
- Morihei Ueshiba

Posted by Mahatma Andy at 00:16

TRAIN ON THE TRAIN

Monday Morning 6th October.

It's a slippery slope this Self Enquiry malarkey. It started off with a few drops of lavender oil in my bath because I was feeling a bit stressed, and now I'm writing a blog about Parabrahman and ego elimination. Commuting is great. An excellent place to train. The practice I use is to send everyone love. Every agitated, angry, sad, happy, beautiful face - love. I shared this technique with one of my Italian gurus - The Iron Goddess - she asked, 'Even the ugly ones?' Even the ugly ones. If you do it right they are no longer ugly. I was practising this on Monday morning because an angry man reminded me to by shoving his very sharp elbows into my ribs. I sent him love, he calmed down.

I sent the rest of the carriage love and all was well. I was remembering Thursday's experience, rooted firmly in the past, trying to figure out how I did it. Going through the head knowledge. It points in the right direction, makes me feel safe.

It is just a decision. Do or not do, there is no try. Ping! I woke up again. Lovely. Walking out of Liverpool Street Station, seeing it for the first time. Such detail. The McDonalds selling its wares 24/7 - no attachment, no aversion. Wonderful peace.

I got that wanderlust feeling again - wanted to roam London just to experience it from this perspective. No attachment, no aversion.

But the mind immediately jumped on that want and told me that would be utterly foolish and to snap out of this nonsense. You are right, Keith. I can feel this anywhere. So I carried on as usual, observing myself going through the motions whilst Keith sulked and subtly worked his black magic to bring me back into the world.

It didn't last as long as the evening session, more distraction, more forms jostling for attention, more ego provocation. I'm definitely getting the hang of it though.

'Spring forth from the Great Earth; Billow like Great Waves; Stand like a tree, sit like a rock; Use One to strike All. Learn and forget!'
- *Morihei Ueshiba*

Posted by Mahatma Andy at 01:32

DEATH

I listened to a friend today - Guru Heart. His wife died yesterday after an eleven month battle with motor neurone disease. Forty years together. He loves her dearly.

Can you remain positive despite what is happening around you?

The last two weeks he sat by her side in hospital, caring for her. Sleeping in the chair beside her bed. Washing her, shaving her legs, cutting her hair, paying particular attention to the back of the neck. He manicured her nails. Perfumed her, polished her glasses - they really suited her. He made her look beautiful. She died looking beautiful. She is beautiful.

Do we die?

Are we the body?

Are we the mind? Yes.

Do we die?

Are we the body?

Are we the mind? No.

Both are right.

'Tell him about your experiences with death, Andy.'

Shut up, Keith, and help me send him love.

'Real love should be the basis of marriage. Real love has no element of needing the other one, or possessing the other one. Real love wants only to make the other one happy.'
- Lester Levenson

WEDNESDAY, 8 OCTOBER 2008
LISTEN TO THE MUSIC

Monday 6th October

Guru Monty entered the room with the guitar held on his shoulder. He strummed an unusual chord sequence and sang his heart out. No discernable words, it was a chant. It was the best piece of music I have ever heard. It was not skilled by western standards, but he put his all into that song, it was from his being.

Learn and forget. Guru Monty will be 2 years old in November.

'Music is the space between the notes.'
- *Claude Debussy*

Space, nothing is important. Nothing is important. Physicists have shown that the human body is almost 100% space. The distance between atoms being so vast compared to their size. And inside the atom there is even more space. Buddhists have known this for 2500 years, Hindus even longer - 5000 years.

Keith thinks this is semantics and a clever word trick and should be dismissed. Keith is right. We shouldn't think about it and label it, because if you label nothing it becomes something and then you lose its pure essence. You should experience nothing instead. Use the words as pointers and experience the peace. Look for the spaces in conversations, in the motion as you walk, in your thoughts, in the music - silence without, stillness within. Enter the space, feel the power and the peace, the silence and the enormous potential.

You will wake up. At first it is subtle, imperceptible. Allow it to expand. Allow yourself to drop it if you get afraid, knowing that it's always there whenever you need it.

I applauded Guru Monty and urged him to play more, as did everyone in the room. He dropped the guitar, scowled as if to say, 'I am not Monkey Boy, that is your lot,' and went off to talk to the fish in the next room. Good lad.

'Ultimately, you must forget about technique.
The further you progress, the fewer teachings there are.
The Great Path is really No Path.'
- Morihei Ueshiba

THURSDAY, 9 OCTOBER 2008
MAYOR OF MONKEY TOWN

Guru Raj was chatting to me about the pull of the world -
'You do enough releasing/meditating and the world becomes
too appealing and this delays making THE decision.'

That is the TRAP. Life becomes effortless, abundant, nothing
is out of reach. Nothing is impossible. But these are worldly
things: baubles, trinkets, fast cars, big houses, attention, ego
inflation. Golden chains.

I'm fed up of being Mayor of Monkey Town, time to go
home.

I read in *Autobiography of a Yogi - Paramhansa Yogananda*:

**'Whenever anyone utters with reverence the name of
Babaji, that devotee attracts an instant spiritual blessing.'**
- Lahiri Mahasaya

and then later that night I meditated on Babaji. A tiny
mosquito started buzzing near my ear. I sent it love as I do
with all insects. They usually leave and bother someone else,
but more recently they have been landing on me to have a
rest. This little beauty landed.

Babaji, Babaji.

I carried on with the meditation and sent it more
love. It had landed between my eyebrows. Babaji, love,
Babaji, love. I felt its proboscis pierce my skin. Babaji, love,
Babaji.

This little feller was having a nice sit down and a cup
of tea. I opened my eyes and could see his out of focus
outline. I laughed. The next morning there was no mark,

gentle creature. The following morning I noticed a small spot where the insect bit. It was the precise middle, exactly inline with the centre of my eyes. Perfect symmetry. Marvellous. Third eye? Meditation point? Some sort of sign? What does it mean? I asked Guru McGod. 'STOP TRYING!' He told me to stop trying to work it out. Ping! All signs are meaningless. It happened, it was interesting to the mind. That's it. Move on.

'You cannot see or touch the Divine with your gross senses. The Divine is within you, not somewhere else.
Unite yourself to the Divine, and you will be able to perceive gods wherever you are, but do not try to grasp or cling to them.'

- Morihei Ueshiba

Posted by Mahatma Andy at 02:07

FRIDAY, 10 OCTOBER 2008
TAKE NOTHING PERSONALLY

Two weeks ago five year-old Guru Star had come around from surgery. Her withered kidney was out and all was well. I joyfully told everyone and the messages of relief and kind wishes came flooding back. Then I received this one: 'Before you tell me how your child is, tell me how sorry you were to hear that mine died.' I phoned to offer my apologies and to explain it was not my intention to cause pain. I listened to a torrent of abuse and anguish, bile, defamation, contempt and condemnation.

Keith was telling me to retaliate and defend, to say all sorts of things to stop the tirade. Shut up, Keith, and help me send her love, can't you hear her pain?

None of the things other people do are because of you. They do them because of themselves. All people live in their own minds, their own dreams; they are in completely different worlds from yours and mine.

If I take things personally then I make the assumption that they know what is in my world. I have no right to try to impose my world on them and theirs.

'If the end result of Illumination is Love, Compassion and Humility, what if we were to do that now?'
— *Robert Adams.*

Posted by Mahatma Andy at 04:31

MONDAY, 13 OCTOBER 2008
PERFECTION

Guru Basil is a perfectionist. He was getting frustrated with his *Lego*. It was his fifth attempt to get the truck roof to stay in position. It just kept coming unstuck. He gave in and asked me for help. I followed the instructions and after four attempts Keith was telling me to throw the truck in the oven and turn the heat up to Gas Mark 8. 'That'll make it stick!'

I decided to apply life lessons to *Lego*. I went back several pages in the manual to see if the foundations were sound. Sure enough, the tiny brick that acts as a keystone was missing. That in place and all was well.

Guru Basil finished playing with his *Lego* and brought me the *Meccano*... I suggested we went for a walk to the park instead.

'Return to that source and leave behind all self-centered thoughts, petty desires, and anger.
Those who are possessed by nothing possess everything.'
- Morihei Ueshiba

Posted by Mahatma Andy at 03:18

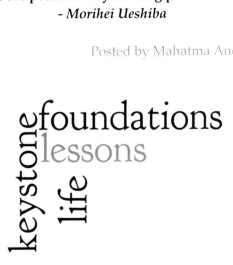

TUESDAY, 14 OCTOBER 2008
JOY

Can you feel it? Just beneath the surface, that feeling of happiness?

> Feel it!
> Let it up, it wants to come up.
> Stop pushing it down with thoughts and worries.
> Feel it.
> Let it up. Go on!

You have no worry big enough to stop it. Nothing in your life is so catastrophic as to keep that feeling down, if you would just recognise it, stop thinking, and let it up. Let it up!

That is your natural self. Everything else is just a projection on that, a cloud covering it. Illusion.

Posted by Mahatma Andy at 01:41

THE ANSWER

Guru Challis asked me this morning if I had got the answer yet. I replied, 'Oh yes - I got that a while back.'

The truth is I always knew it. It had never left me. I'd just forgotten and covered it up with a lot of stuff. And I still do. I get glimpses then get distracted. The pull of the world is very real. Like a dog digging for a bone, sees a cat and chases it. I have yet to see a dog catch a cat. It's almost as if they don't want to.

Guru Basil couldn't sleep last night; he was fighting it all the way. So we did some 'Imagination'. We lay down and let go of the body, and let the mind chatter, let the thoughts come up and watched them.

'Don't think of an elephant!' And the elephant appeared and we watched it. And then we soared off into the Universe and pretended to swallow all the planets into our bodies, then the Sun and the stars, then the Milky Way and the galaxies, until there was nothing left. And we sat in the silence, knowing that everything was inside us. We didn't have to be concerned about the past or worry about the future, we were enjoying the now.

'I'm in the now, Daddy.'

'How do you feel?'

'Relaxed and sleepy.'

He had stopped chasing his cat, stopped digging for his bone. He was himself. Love.

'One does not need buildings, money, power, or status to practice the Art of Peace. Heaven is right where you are standing, and that is the place to train.'
- *Morihei Ueshiba*

Posted by Mahatma Andy at 00:30

WEDNESDAY, 15 OCTOBER 2008
THE TRUTH

The Truth never changes. Anything that changes is a lie. There is a popular belief that the atoms in your body turn over on average every seven years.

So, very few atoms in your body, if any, are original. And yet you look much the same and you can remember things from your childhood.

The body is a lie. People change their minds all the time. The mind is a lie.

The World changes constantly. The World is a lie. This is very comforting because if you know something is a lie it should no longer offend you. But most people let it. Keith thinks I am just being clever with words. He is right again. Because words change, ideas change and they are a lie too.

But all lies point to the Truth. So use them as a guide and experience the Truth. Don't talk about the Truth too much, or write about it, or think about it, or dance about it too much. Experience it.

'The key to good technique is to keep your hands, feet, and hips straight and centered. If you are centered, you can move freely. The physical center is your belly; if your mind is set there as well, you are assured of victory in any endeavor.'

- Morihei Ueshiba

SATURDAY, 18 OCTOBER 2008
STUFF

KISS. Keep It Simple Seeker.

Wanting stuff, trinkets, baubles, gadgets. The latest thing.

For men the stereotype is fast cars and expensive watches, for women - shoes and chocolate.

It is the wanting that is the problem.

Wanting keeps you from having.

You cannot want and have at the same time.

Stop wanting and start having.

The truth is - you have everything.

When a want is satisfied you feel happy. You get a promotion, a new car, the diamonds, the recognition, that film deal. But this happiness does not last, and you want again, to be happy again.

The next want needs to be bigger to get the same hit. You achieve it, feel happy, happiness wanes and so the downward spiral progresses.

Like a drug addict forever craving that one last fix.

Why not be happy all the time?

If you get in touch with your true nature, you actually stop wanting.

You begin to know the happiness that you really are is far more intense, satisfying and wonderful than the happiness you could feel from worldly achievements.

You could suddenly become the richest person in the world by inventing the chocolate shoe. (An item that confuses women into remaining silent and peaceful by focusing the chattering mind on the question, 'Should I eat it or wear it?') But the happiness felt would still only be a small glimpse of what is available, of what you really are, if you would only remove the clouds of the world illusion. So why not concentrate on getting in touch with the happiness inside and leave alone the spiral trap of worldly wanting? Why not have happiness constantly no matter what happens in the world?

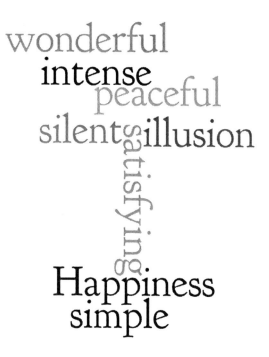

'Truth is very simple. A flower does not try to be beautiful. It's True Nature is Beauty. It exudes fragrance, beauty, perfection. Just by its very Being. In the same way, when you Awaken to your True Nature You will naturally exude Love, Compassion, Beauty. It is all you. For it is your True Self.'

- *Robert Adams*

MONDAY, 27 OCTOBER 2008
TREE HUGGING

I went to a tree hugging seminar at the weekend.

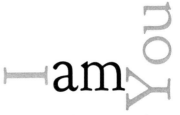

It was well attended - sign of the times. There I met Guru Billy - another Scot. We were releasing on worry and really powering through the exercise, incredible energy rising. We both became worry free very quickly and were wondering what to do next with the remaining thirty minutes.

'What is stopping you from being free all the time, Andy?'

'My mind, Billy.'

'Why don't you be free now? Like you said in your Love letter. Right now.'

I felt a rush. Keith kicked in straight away. Confusion. Real horrible crippling confusion. Rabbit in the headlights. Panic.

'You can't go free in front of him! It's bad enough that you do it quietly on your own. He'll think you're an idiot, a hippy tree hugger, or worse, a fake. You will look really stupid. What're you going to do to prove that you are free? Levitate? Shine like a God? You left your halo at home. You'll have to prove it to him. Or he won't believe you. And then you will be scorned. Don't look into his eyes. Look away!'

Frustration, tears rising, terrible fear. Terror. Then laughter at the stupidity of it all. Push through the joy, because that is another trap. Look into Billy's eyes.

Now! You can do it.

'Don't you dare! He is a freak, he's worse than you. Look at the way he releases, all serious and full of himself. He's a fraud, too. Don't look into his eyes! Don't!'

I let Keith have his rant and then calmly looked into Billy's eyes. And there I was staring back.

I am you, Billy. Peace.

'Peace is non-resistance, complete acceptance, identification with all, everyone, everything.'
- *Lester Levenson*

Posted by Mahatma Andy at 01:30

TUESDAY, 28 OCTOBER 2008
THE WORLD

Guru Monty went climbing yesterday. He is very good for a two year-old (One year, eleven months to be exact). He is also very quick. And I couldn't get to him before he fell off the sofa and bumped his head on the floor. He started to cry with the pain. *In The Night Garden* was on the TV - he noticed Iggle Piggle jumping up and down and dancing. So he decided to stop crying, start laughing and join in the dance.

The world has been with us forever.

There will be calamities.

It is not going to get any worse, and it is not going to get any better.

How you think of these things determines what happens to you. In this world pain is unavoidable but suffering is optional. If you step on a cat's paw it hisses and spits for a couple of seconds, and gets out of the way. It doesn't bitch and moan for forty years and hold a grudge against you.

The world exists to train you, to polish your spirit, to draw you higher, to make you shine. How you do anything is how you do everything.

Fall over seven times, stand up and dance eight.

'You will be on this earth a short while. Everything that you do determines your state of consciousness, what you will experience. Be very careful to surround yourself with Truth. Discern wisely.'
- *Robert Adams*

Posted by Mahatma Andy at 00:57

WEDNESDAY, 29 OCTOBER 2008
SIN

'Let he who is without sin cast the first stone.'

So if the Virgin Mary rocked up and launched a piece of flint right between your eyes, would that count? Or if Jesus decided to have a go would that be a fall from grace? Everyone has sinned, does that include Mary and Jesus?

And so the arguments rage. You can see the futility of over-thinking the message, debating the scriptures, as words are inadequate. We end up missing the point. Better to understand the sentiment, the chord it strikes within. The answer you get from the silence.

Keith thinks I am a big sinner and stones me regularly. He can't forgive, he can't forget. He's a rascal. A devil. The beatings don't come as often now, and when they do they are not as severe. This is because I've learnt to treat him with love and compassion.

'So many come to me that talk about love and peace, that know all of the great quotes, that pride themselves on their spiritual knowledge. Yet they are the meanest people that you will ever meet. They say the meanest, nastiest things about other people. They do not understand the laws of correct living. These actions transgress the laws of happiness. And so it goes on. Until we realise the Truth. That everything we say and do will have repercussions. That not only are we the part and parcel of Supreme Love, Supreme All Perfect Reality, All Embracing Compassion, but so is everyone else. And we treat them as such.'

- Robert Adams

'Be gentle with yourself.' *- Guru McGod*

THURSDAY, 30 OCTOBER 2008
HENDRIX

Guru Jimi was telling me this morning how he likes to stand up next to a mountain and chop it down with the edge of his hand.

I know how he feels. He once told me that he has been imitated so well that he has heard people copy his mistakes. Jimi has made some beautiful mistakes, I am so glad he didn't get it right the first time.

I was trying to copy Hendrix last night on my *Epiphone Les Paul*. I can't get anywhere near his mistakes.
Jimi laughs at this, as he finds he can't get anywhere near my mistakes either - not just the musical ones.

Keith says I should be using a Gibson at least and not a cheap copy, and that anyway, Jimi used a Strat. If you must use an Epiphone use the vintage FT79 acoustic guitar that Hendrix used for song writing in the late 1960s, like the one that was sold at auction in 2001 for $77,000.

I refuse to blame my axe.

'I don't give a fuck if you boo, as long as you boo in key.'
- *Jimi Hendrix*

Posted by Mahatma Andy at 02:10

FRIDAY, 31 OCTOBER 2008
PUNCH IN THE FACE

Mike Tyson said, 'Everyone thinks they have a plan until they get punched in the face.' He is good at what he does because he keeps going despite the blows. Have you noticed in life that you are happy one moment and then get punched in the face for no apparent reason? People say nasty, terrible, untrue things about you. Or something goes wrong with that foolproof plan. Or seventy million people die in two world wars.

Man's inhumanity to man. You try to rationalise it and you become lost and confused. You grow heavier and entangled. Everything becomes hopeless. Why go on? You stop trying. You give up. And then in the darkest hour you relinquish control. That is when it happens. You see a glimpse of your true nature. Love, compassion and humility. You rise. And you talk about your new found land to others because you want them to have it too.

But they have their problems, ideas and troubles. Most don't believe you. They don't believe there is such a magnificent place, there is only what they see; pain and scant hurried patches of pleasure. It makes them mad that you are happy. So they try to drag you down into the dark world of troubles. And it works. The cycle of blind suffering. Then something clicks. You see the cycle. You see you are not dead. You see the illusion, the daymare. You give up the cycle in one simple decision. You don't wait for the weekend to do it. Or for next year when you'll be made Chief Under Manager of Corporateness. Or for when the Queen recommends your genius as an undergarment maker. You do it now. From moment to moment. Forever. You are home.

Posted by Mahatma Andy at 03:28

MONDAY, 3 NOVEMBER 2008
FEAR OF DYING

All problems stem from the fear of dying. Not just the terrifying fear of your own death but also of the people around you. If we could be guaranteed we do not die, that we've never been born, and we just exist in love, peace and bliss forever - would we be worried about anything? Would we have any problems? Probably. Keith could find many ways. He does pretty well already. Despite all the evidence, he still insists that we die. Guru Adams once said to me that it was a mistake to think you can solve any major problems just with potatoes. Doug was right. So, whenever I have a problem I always ask if I can solve it with just potatoes. If I can't then I know I've got a major problem. It also helps me get things in perspective. That one moment of ridiculousness helps me see the reality.

There are no problems. Everything is perfect. Exactly how it should be. I didn't think it was perfect when my father died. And I don't think that now. I'm not sure I can ever think that my father dying was in any way perfect.

But if we never die, we are never born, and we exist in love, peace and bliss. Eternal. And if the only reason we don't see this is because we are looking at a mud-caked window, then I am willing to try to open that window and see my father looking back. I bet he's holding a potato and wants to use that mud to make it grow. Marvellous sense of humour.

'Do not look upon this world with fear and loathing. Bravely face whatever the gods offer. '
- *Morihei Ueshiba*

Posted by Mahatma Andy at 01:14

TUESDAY, 4 NOVEMBER 2008
STORIES

It is important to take yourself off automatic. Break up a routine and think for yourself. Don't always follow the herd. Everything can be considered a cult, a form of programming. Not just the more colourful creeds, but all religions, western society, communism, capitalism, any regime of thought.

Guru Taleb suggested I give up reading newspapers and stop listening to the news on TV. Any important bit of news will come to you. For the last three years Taleb's advice has proved to be very good. My life has become less cluttered.

I notice the 'free' newspapers being given out on the London streets. All those people receiving a limited point of view.

I hope they can discriminate. What if every idea has been thought before? What if it has all been done before? Hindu scriptures talked about the big bang and relativity 7000 years before Einstein. It just might have all been done before.

It is a simple premise, the Truth never changes. Ergo, everything that changes is a lie. This world is a lie, the body is a lie, the mind is a lie. Einstein's theories are lies. Any thought regime is a lie. I've always been seeking some deeper meaning. It has always been there in the background. Gently encouraging me to look.

My family was non-religious but I used to attend Sunday School by choice from the age of seven. I enjoyed the stories and the simple messages, but quickly realised the futility of man controlling man. I trained as a scientist, a magician, a stand up comedian, I studied the occult. I became an atheist, until Richard Dawkins persuaded me not to be an atheist with his excellent book *The God Delusion*.

I am turning more spiritual now, but still non-religious.

It has been a very interesting journey. A journey that has been done before. Many times before.

'Basically... out of all the ridiculous religion stories—which are greatly, wonderfully ridiculous—the silliest one I've ever heard is, 'Yeah... there's this big giant universe and it's expanding, it's all gonna collapse on itself and we're all just here just 'cause... just cause. That, to me, is the most ridiculous explanation ever.'

- Trey Parker

Posted by Mahatma Andy at 00:12

TIME

Time is an illusion. All the clues are there. Even scientists are starting to realise.

You've got to love scientists; solve one problem by coming up with ten more. Busy, busy, busy.

I read an article by the lead scientist, Carlo Rovelli, he says:

'It is not reality that has a time flow, it is our very approximate knowledge of reality that has a time flow. Time is the effect of our ignorance.' Beautiful. Buddha could not have said it better.

Reinventing the wheel, though. It has all been done before. Or as time does not exist, it has all been thought, done, improved upon instantaneously. And then redone, rethought, re-improved - ad infinitum. Even that statement implies time, but leads closer to the truth.

The concept of time is a limitation. Once you get rid of that limitation amazing things should begin to happen. Teleportation, prescience, omnipresence, you will never die and you can never be born.

Keith says that was a step too far. 'Where's the proof in the literature? At least the scientists are trying to put it in concrete terms. They are trying to understand it, you are spouting nonsense.'

I say if you get rid of another limitation, e.g., thinking, then you will be there. Stop thinking and start experiencing.

We've all done it. Waiting for Christmas as a child. The conversations my mum had with her friends on the way to the shops, would they ever stop? Kissing my wife for the first time, seems like yesterday.

But that is not it either; those moments are again just pointers to the Truth.

Be still. Breathe in and say to yourself, 'I', breathe out and say 'Am'. Do this for a day.

I'll do it myself when I get the time. Over to Guru Adams again:

'Time is an illusion. Lunchtime doubly so.'
- Douglas Adams

'There is a theory which states that if ever anybody discovers exactly what the Universe is for and why it is here, it will instantly disappear and be replaced by something even more bizarre and inexplicable. There is another theory which states that this has already happened.'

- Douglas Adams

Posted by Mahatma Andy at 00:00

WEDNESDAY, 5 NOVEMBER 2008
FREEDOM

'When I had my awakening, I was fourteen years old. This body was sitting in a classroom taking a math test. And all of a sudden I felt myself expanding. I never left my body, which proves that the body never existed to begin with. I felt the body expanding, and a brilliant light began to come out of my heart. I happened to see the light in all directions. I had peripheral vision, and this light was really my Self. It was not my body and the light. There were not two. There was this light that became brighter and brighter and brighter, the light of a thousand suns. I thought I would be burnt to a crisp, but alas, I wasn't.

But this brilliant light, of which I was the center and also the circumference, expanded throughout the universe, and I was able to feel the planets, the stars, the galaxies, as myself. And this light shone so bright, yet it was beautiful, it was bliss, it was ineffable, indescribable.

After a while the light began to fade away, and there was no darkness. There was just a place between light and darkness, the place beyond the light. You can call it the void, but it wasn't just a void. It was this Pure Awareness I always talk about. I was aware that I Am That I Am. I was aware of the whole universe at the same time. There was no time, there was no space, there was just the I Am.

Then everything began to return to normal, so to speak. I was able to feel and understand that all of the planets, the galaxies, the people, the trees, the flowers on this earth, everything, were myriads of energy, and I was in everything. I was the flower. I was the sky. I was the people. The I was everything. Everything was the I. The word 'I' encompassed the whole universe.'

- Robert Adams

**'Remember when you were young, you shone like the sun.
Shine on you crazy diamond.'**
- Roger Waters

Posted by Mahatma Andy at 23:34

FRIDAY, 7 NOVEMBER 2008
PARADISE

The Bureau of Meteorology in Australia runs a photographic competition each year, looking at some of these images got me thinking:

This world may be an illusion but it can be a very beautiful one. Can be an absolute shocker, too. Keith doesn't fancy getting caught in the lightning strike in Darwin. He can moan about every single picture on that calendar; that sea looks cold. Imagine spending the night there. Fire!

It is so easy to get caught up in the world. So many distractions. Beautiful and bad.

If you were living a fairly comfortable life in a village, experiencing the usual ups-and-downs, triumphs and disappointments, joy of birth, the sadness of death, good health and crippling disease, and you knew that just outside that village, across the Swamp of Doom, lay Paradise where there was nothing but bliss, would you make the journey?

Depends what is in the Swamp of Doom.

But if you knew you could not die you wouldn't care what was in the swamp. And you'd walk into Paradise.

That pesky fear of dying again.

So that's the key:

Know that you never die.

Be prepared to put up with a bit of unpleasantness for a while.

I'm having trouble with the first bit.

And the second if I'm honest.

But my rational brain is saying that I am conditioning myself with mumbo jumbo. It concedes that I have never been happier and lighter in my life despite what is going on around me. It also concedes that fundamentally I haven't changed and it is beginning to realise that my substratum is in fact happiness.

I have a choices:

1. Get involved in the world and try to conquer and bend everything to my will.

or

2. Keep going, keep practising my releasing, meditation, self enquiry, developing love, compassion and humility and getting happier and lighter.

I choose Paradise.

'When Alexander of Macedonia was thirty-three he cried salt tears because there were no more worlds to conquer-Bristow is only twenty-seven.'
- Sid Waddell

Posted by Mahatma Andy at 00:21

paradise

choose

MONDAY, 10 NOVEMBER 2008
INSTRUCTORS

I like to visit the Art of Peace site for an inspirational quote.

Today I clicked on:

'Instructors can impart only a fraction of the teaching. It is through your own devoted practice that the mysteries of the Art of Peace are brought to life.'

This is something I keep coming back to recently.

You can read up on a subject until you are a walking encyclopaedia, you can have all the head knowledge in the world, but eventually you have to apply it, you have to experience the subject.

This is the problem of the world, so many people reading and talking about it, few actually doing something about it. This has always been the world's problem.

What did I do today to get myself to realise the Truth? Did I sit and moan about something that happened thirty years ago? Did I read a newspaper and tut at man's inhumanity to man? Did I sit and 'relax' in the evening by watching someone else's problems on a soap opera? Did I go to the pub and get slightly high on European fighting lager?

Or did I sit and use the mind to conquer the mind?

Did I ask the awkward questions?

Who am I?

What is this world?

To whom do these thoughts come?

What am I?

What is my relation to the world?

Did I let the answers come to me?

Did I try to control the answers, so that they conformed to the answers that I had read about?

Or did I sit and wait?

Ask the questions and sit in the silence.

I decided to give myself a treat and to see if Guru Ueshiba has any advice on what I have just written, so I clicked on the grid once more:

'It is necessary to develop a strategy that utilizes all the physical conditions and elements that are directly at hand. The best strategy relies upon an unlimited set of responses.'

Spot on again! I am now going to post a random quote from the interweb, this one from www.random-quotes.com:

'I wish there was a knob on the TV to turn up the intelligence. There's a knob called `brightness', but it doesn't work.'
- *Gallagher*

Posted by Mahatma Andy at 09:35

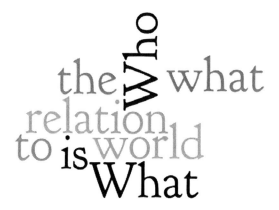

TUESDAY, 11 NOVEMBER 2008
IGNIS FATUUS

I read a very long article about Wall Street today.

The author Michael Lewis is a good, persuasive writer and he managed to draw me into his Maya illusion. I felt quite sick after reading about the excesses of capitalism. Then I started to discriminate:

So, a few swearing nerds made a lot of money from the collapse of the global financial system, and a large man with big hands lost a job that was well paid because of some words that were written about him and the empire he created. What does that mean?

If you take it from the view point of leaving the world alone, of realising the illusion then it means nothing. Absolutely meaningless.

My granny wouldn't have a frame of reference to understand that Michael Lewis article; it would take some time to explain it to her, to get her to appreciate the complexity of the illusion. In fact, I'm not sure you could explain that one to my gran, she'd probably look blankly and say, 'That's nice, dear.' But get her talking about homosexuality, or black presidents and that would be a different matter.

Nothing matters. No thing matters.

What is beyond matter is what matters. Things, stuff, illusion, complexity, trash it, it is all worthless. Foolish fire, *Ignis Fatuus*.

If you have nothing and everyone around you loses their stuff, are you in a better situation?

If you have nothing then you are in the best position of all, and you would rejoice at everyone else having nothing. But of course this is hard to understand as most people are involved in this *Ignis Fatuus* that is the world.

'Those who are possessed by nothing possess everything.'
- *Morihei Ueshiba*

WEDNESDAY, 12 NOVEMBER 2008
HIVE MIND

Most people baulk at the idea that humans have a hive mind. They have a deep fear of losing their identity. They want to be an individual. They want separation. They want an ego.

A type of hive mind is conformity. Attitudes, beliefs, and behaviours are influenced by other people. Responses may occur as the result of subtle influences, or by direct and overt social pressure. Conformity may also occur because of the 'implied presence' of others, when other people are not actually present. Religions are good at instilling this implied presence. This want of separation causes a lot of unhappiness.

Here's a good exercise: Look at a stranger in the street and say to yourself, 'You are me.' Do it and see what happens. What is wrong with admitting we all have the same needs, desires, worries, fears, and thoughts?

Nothing.

BRIAN COHEN OF NAZARETH:
Look, you've got it all wrong! You don't need to follow me! You don't need to follow anybody! You've got to think for yourselves! You're all individuals!

CROWD:
Yes, we're all individuals!
Brian Cohen of Nazareth:
You're all different!
CROWD:
Yes, we are all different!
HOMOGENOUS MAN:
I'm not.
CROWD:
Shhh!

Script excerpt - Monty Python's *The Life of Brian*

Posted by Mahatma Andy at 07:24

THURSDAY, 13 NOVEMBER 2008
NOTHING IS GOING ON

I was introduced to this marvellous concept the other day: Nothing is happening, nothing is going on.

Time, the world, the planets, the universe are all illusion, like a dream, and your experiences, emotions and energy are all hallucinatory. When you dream it seems so real. Years can pass in a dream. You can go grow old, fly, breathe underwater, become young again - fantastic feats and it all seems so reasonable.

You can also have horrors - incredible fears and vile monsters. When you wake up you realise the deception. The idea is that there are many layers of this deception. The Truth is nothing is going on. It's a lovely concept; just thinking deeply on it makes you feel happy. Try it. Keith says it makes him scared. You have to do something, you have to be someone, you must survive. Keith is a lot quieter nowadays but this idea woke him up.

So, all the meditation, reading of scriptures, going to church, raves, all the things you do to get high is a waste of time. Any peak experience has not actually happened. Any gain, any loss. Nothing has happened. Just peace. Bliss beyond imagination. And so to the random quote generator to sum up the above:

'I believe in an open mind,
but not so open that your brains fall out.'
- *Arthur Hays Sulzberger*

MONDAY, 17 NOVEMBER 2008
REINCARNATION

I had a dream. In this dream I was a hermit meditating all day long. A great sage came by my spot. He was off to see God. So I asked him to ask God how long I would have to sit meditating to become enlightened.

When he returned he told me to look at the big, leafy tree I was sitting under and to count the leaves. That was how many lifetimes I would have to reincarnate before I became enlightened. I grew angry. I had been meditating all my life. I thought, 'Sod that! I don't even believe in reincarnation, I didn't the first time I was here.' I got up and went into town to get drunk and chase some skirt. The next moment I was under the tree again meditating and the great sage walked by, off to see God. I asked him to ask God how long it would be until I was enlightened.

When he returned he told me to count the leaves on the tree again, and that was how many lifetimes I would have to reincarnate before I became enlightened.

This time I jumped up and down with joy and shouted, 'Thank you God, just one tree!'

I woke up laughing.

'The techniques of the Art of Peace are neither fast nor slow, nor are they inside or outside. They transcend time and space.'
- *Morihei Ueshiba*

TUESDAY, 18 NOVEMBER 2008
THE WORLD IS NOT AN ILLUSION

The only thing that is constant in this world is change. Everything changes.

Perfect Truth would never change. So everything that changes is a lie, an illusion?

The world is *not* an illusion.

This is a concept.

The world *is* an illusion.

This is another concept.

What would absolute reality have to do with concepts?

Nothing.

The Truth is already there, why would it need a general incomplete idea about itself? It doesn't. So both concepts must be wrong. Illusions if you like.

Keith is complaining. Clever incomplete argument. It's not even clever, just confusing and not at all helpful. Taking things to the limit is not satisfying.

Tell that to Newton, Einstein, Feynman, all of them loved their calculus and taking things to the limit.

And Keith again is right.

My argument is wrong. In fact in absolute reality it doesn't exist. How can it? The world cannot exist, I can't exist, so how can my musings exist?

They can't.

So why bother writing a blog of nonsense? To prove to myself that collating facts, reading books, learning, debating, musing is not the way to find the answer. It points the way. But there comes a time when you have to forget.

Learn and forget.

And the way is beyond thought. Have you tried to stop thinking? It is lovely.

'Move like a beam of light:
Fly like lightning,
Strike like thunder,
Whirl in circles around
A stable center.'
- *Morihei Ueshiba*

MONDAY, 24 NOVEMBER 2008
SERVICE

It is extremely rare for an individual to give up identifying with the body and be of service to everyone. Mother Teresa and Ghandi are two such that spring to mind. Oh yeah, and Bono.

Another name for service is love. Not the claustrophobic you are mine to the exclusion of all others human love, but all encompassing divine love. Whenever I have done something to help another without expecting anything in return it has been an almost absent-minded service, no thought involved, just a compunction to be there for that person. I have always been amazed what an incredible feeling of happiness I derive from it. The benefit to me has always outweighed the potential hardship of being there. Why don't I do this continually? Like Teresa and Ghandi. I don't believe I'm good enough. I don't believe in myself.

How can I make your life better today? That is how I should greet everybody. Best make a start; I've wasted a lot of time.

'The Art of Peace does not rely on weapons or brute force to succeed; instead we put ourselves in tune with the universe, maintain peace in our own realms, nurture life, and prevent death and destruction. The true meaning of the term samurai is one who serves and adheres to the power of love.'

- Morihei Ueshiba

TUESDAY, 25 NOVEMBER 2008
SPACE

I was musing with Guru Basil about space. Science has proven that the human body is almost entirely made up of space. This is due to the incredibly small size of the molecules/atoms and the vast distances between them. Intriguing thought.

Guru Basil helped me out:

'It makes sense, Dad. We are part of the Earth, the Earth is part of the solar system, the sun, the stars, which are all part of the galaxies, which are all part of space. It is all connected.'

He instantly saw it and took it to another level.

Einstein would be proud.

And Eddington.

Eddington did the measurements that put Einstein and his theories on the world map. Eddington had a strong belief in God.

My guess is that science and religion will eventually realise they are seeing the same thing.

'Science without religion is lame.
Religion without science is blind.'
- Albert Einstein

'A human being is a part of a whole, called by us universe, a part limited in time and space. He experiences himself, his thoughts and feelings as something separated from the rest... a kind of optical delusion of his consciousness. This delusion is a kind of prison for us, restricting us to our personal desires and to affection for a few persons nearest to us. Our task must be to free ourselves from this prison by widening our circle of compassion to embrace all living creatures and the whole of nature in its beauty.'

- Albert Einstein

Posted by Mahatma Andy at 06:10

WEDNESDAY, 26 NOVEMBER 2008
BRUSSEL SPROUTS

When I was fourteen I worked in a fruit and veg shop three evenings a week, after school for two hours, and all day Saturday.

Guru Nana used to bring me ½ lb of *Jelly Babies* every Saturday afternoon. She would stand outside the shop not wanting to disturb the bustle. In the evenings I would visit her and she would bathe my feet in a *Radox* salt bath and feed me angel cake and copious cups of tea. Guru Granddad would talk about space, time, infinity and crosswords.

Wonderful.

One Saturday afternoon when it was quiet in the shop I was out the back sorting the 'snotty' Brussels sprouts from the good ones. Not an interesting or pleasant task. So I started thinking about a question Granddad had asked me:

'Can you imagine infinity?'

I gave it a go.

The next thing I knew I was being shaken by the shop owner, asking me if I was OK. Apparently I had been staring into space for the last forty-five minutes, snotty sprout in hand. They had decided to leave me at first because I looked funny, but after a while they grew concerned.

I was fine. Very fine.

I could remember nothing about the experience. Just the decision to let go and think of infinity. I was trying to reach the end of the universe. I didn't get there. I explained all this to the people in the shop who looked concerned. They started to look even more concerned, so I decided to keep quiet and never try it again.

It was a lovely experience but tainted by wanting the approval of the people present. I'm going to give it another go tonight, Brussels sprouts are in season.

'We kids feared many things in those days - werewolves, dentists, North Koreans, Sunday School - but they all paled in comparison with Brussels sprouts.'
- *Dave Barry, Miami Herald Columnist*

Posted by Mahatma Andy at 09:40

EXERCISE

Guru Monty decided to join me for morning exercise. He woke up early and grumpy. He wanted to be held as he is only two years-old and likes the security.

Don't we all? Nothing wrong with having security, it is the wanting it that causes the suffering.

The problem was I wanted to exercise. So I did both. I held Monty and tailored my routine to incorporate a giggling bundle of glee. We had a lot of fun. Bouncing up and down, running on the spot, stretching, swinging, ducking, diving. He has joined me three mornings in a row now.

Now the problem comes now when I try to leave for work. He wants to come. Tears and clinging, pleading to go with me. I hand him back to mum. And leave.

That is the hard bit.

I ask mum how long he cries for after I leave.

About two seconds and then he is off playing music or he starts colouring.

Life goes on.

'Daily training in the Art of Peace allows your inner divinity to shine brighter and brighter. Do not concern yourself with the right and wrong of others. Do not be calculating or act unnaturally. Keep your mind set on the Art of Peace, and do not criticize other teachers or traditions. The Art of Peace never restrains, restricts, or shackles anything. It embraces all and purifies everything.'

- Morihei Ueshiba

Posted by Mahatma Andy at 05:35

MONDAY, 1 DECEMBER 2008
CONSCIOUSNESS

Everything has a consciousness, buildings, trees, people, animals. Everything. Everything affects your thinking. Everything affects your action. Everything affects your being. So keep good company and natural surroundings.

Reminds me of pigeons. The ones seen in London compared to the ones seen in the country. Feet missing, misshapen, oily, tufted feathers, scratching at filthy pavements compared to the well- groomed specimens hanging out in the woods dining on the finest grub. Why don't these unhappy pigeons move to the country? They are probably not unhappy. And they are not thinking. They are just going through the motions of existence. London isn't bad, it just may not be the most natural habitat for most people.

I've always thought that for meditation to be any good you must be able to do it anywhere and at any time. Not just for thirty minutes in the mornings and evenings but twenty-four hours a day, seven days a week. Not just in a nice warm room, scented with candles and permeated with relaxing music, but also in the heat of a war zone, scented with cordite and permeated with explosions.

SAS Meditators - that would be an interesting regiment. A platoon of soldiers floating around a war zone telling everyone to pack it in. London could be the training ground.

'Rely on Peace To activate your Manifold powers; Pacify your environment. And create a beautiful world.'
- *Morihei Ueshiba*

Posted by Mahatma Andy

WEDNESDAY, 3 DECEMBER 2008
THE DOOR

'When I was a child, my parents told me never to open the cellar door. 'Never open the cellar door,' they said, and for many years, I obeyed them, although I always wondered what it was that was so dangerous behind the cellar door. And then one day, when there was no one around, I finally got up my courage... I slowly walked over... I put out my hand... and I opened the cellar door. And I saw wonderful things! Amazing things! Trees! The sky! Other children!'

- Emo Phillips

That is one of my favourite jokes.

One day you wish to do more than look out of the door. You stop listening to the people around you, the people who mean well but have become lost and want the safety in numbers. You listen to your heart, your true self. And you realise you must get up, brush yourself off, leave behind all that held you in darkness, the anger, the rage, resentment, self-pity, meanness and leave the basement. You simply pick up your feet and get on with it. You walk out the door.

'You cannot see or touch the Divine with your gross senses. The Divine is within you, not somewhere else. Unite yourself to the Divine, and you will be able to perceive gods wherever you are, but do not try to grasp or cling to them.'

- Morihei Ueshiba

Posted by Mahatma Andy at 01:30

FRIDAY, 5 DECEMBER 2008
BETTY

Betty died yesterday. And Boris started eating her corpse. The kids were distraught. Tropical fish are beautiful creatures.

'I hate that crab Boris! Why do we have to have him?' cried Guru Basil. Guru Star was wailing. 'Cruel, cruel crab!' Guru Monty looked bemused and started playing the harmonica. I explained that Betty decided to leave her body and didn't need it any more. It sank to the bottom of the tank and Boris didn't know any better and thought he'd eat it to keep his body strong, after all Betty didn't need it anymore. Don't judge Boris, he didn't kill Betty.

That seemed to work. But I am waiting for the cannibal questions.

'Techniques employ four qualities that reflect the nature of our world. Depending on the circumstance, you should be: hard as a diamond, flexible as a willow, smooth-flowing like water, or as empty as space.'
- Morihei Ueshiba

Posted by Mahatma Andy at 03:16

TUESDAY, 9 DECEMBER 2008
PEACE

I saw Guru Irene this weekend. She seems to have finally found peace. She has that look in her eyes. Distant, but the lights are on and the mind is still very sharp. It wasn't always that way. She battled alcoholism for twenty years and it crippled her. Her mind was dulled and railing against everything in those years. It has left her gaunt, twisted and in pain. She hardly eats, she shuffles about on a *Zimmer* frame, and finds little joy in the world now. Even her grandchildren fail to drag her back into the illusion. She has had enough. But she has found peace.

Have you?

I asked her what she has learnt in her time on this earth.

'Be tough, be strong, don't let others push you about.'

I love you, Irene. You are me.

'Study the teachings of the pine tree, the bamboo, and the plum blossom. The pine is evergreen, firmly rooted, and venerable. The bamboo is strong, resilient, unbreakable. The plum blossom is hardy, fragrant, and elegant.'
- *Morihei Ueshiba*

THURSDAY, 11 DECEMBER 2008
FLOYD

Looking back I think my school was trying to tell me something. All the teachers had comical names. Mr Carpenter, the woodwork teacher, Mrs French, the French teacher and Mrs Spatula, the Home Economics teacher. I made that last one up, but the others are true.

In 1979 Pink Floyd's *Another Brick in the Wall* was a hit in Britain, and was causing controversy. I was thirteen and the English teacher, Mrs Semi-Colon, asked us to write an essay on it. Mine was read out. I argued that the song was just as bad as the institution it was railing against. Its monotonous hypnotic beat inciting kids to rise up and change the system. A popular idea with the teachers but not popular with the kids. So I got the usual wedgie in the playground and when I took my duffle coat off at home I wondered where all the phlegm on the back of it had come from. I think I was trying to say 'Leave the world alone'. I knew deep down it was pointless trying to change it. It won't get any worse it won't get any better. It is just a test.

I lost sight of that as I grew into adulthood, hypnotised by my surroundings. You can only be hypnotised if you want to be hypnotised. I don't want to be hypnotised anymore. Time to wake up.

**'If you don't eat yer meat, you can't have any pudding!
How can you have any pudding if you don't eat yer meat?!'
- *Roger Waters***

Posted by Mahatma Andy at 01:05

MONDAY, 22 DECEMBER 2008
PINK KINK IN YOUR THINK

It's drawing in.

I can feel it. Any moment now I will lose my mind and I'll be in bliss. Not just when I try hard for a couple of hours but all the time. I know it. And it scares me.

I find distractions. Picking arguments, watching television, movies, provoking people, judging, getting involved in pointless conversations. Ego stuff. Anything but to sit still and observe. Keith is back on the scene, making me doubt.

'You'll lose everything. Your job, wife (and she'll take the children.) Have you noticed you are annoying other people? Making them feel uncomfortable. They say things behind your back. They think you strange. You are no longer one of them. It's not too late; you can go back to your old ways.'

Old ways? No thanks. I'm prepared to lose everything. I think. And that's the problem. I think I'm prepared, but not sure. I think. That's the problem. I think.

But when I'm quiet I know that I will lose nothing and gain everything. I need to be quiet more often. All the time. No one is annoyed by the caring quiet man listening to their problems.

I need a Jackalope to remind me to keep Boundin'.

'The Art of Peace is not easy. It is a fight to the finish, the slaying of evil desires and all falsehood within. On occasion the Voice of Peace resounds like thunder, jolting human beings out of their stupor.'

- Morihei Ueshiba

MONDAY, 2 FEBRUARY 2009
PARABRAHMAN

There is no mind, no body, no world, no universe, no God, no karma, no past lives, no samskaras and no parabrahman. None of this exists.

You have to come to terms with your life. That takes total honesty. You can't go on fooling yourself. Look how you run around from pillar to post. You go here, you go there. You are always searching. You are always looking. You are always striving. For what?

Some of you think you are going to find a teacher up in the sky some place, that you are going to go searching for that teacher until you find him or her. No such teacher exists. When you finally settle down and start going into the Silence more often, the teacher will appear to you and you will find he is none other than yourself.

I am yourself. I can see that very clearly. There is no difference between you and me. When you feel depressed, when you feel angry, when you feel out of sorts, that's me you feel. When you feel happy, when you feel enlightened, when you feel beautiful, that is also me you feel. All this is the Self, and I am That. You still think I'm talking about Mahatma Andy? Mahatma Andy has nothing to do with this.

I'm speaking of Omnipresence. I'm speaking of nothing. And I think to continue writing is a waste of time. Good luck.

'The divine beauty
Of heaven and earth!
All creation,
Members of
One family.'
- *Morihei Ueshiba*

THE END

THE
BEGINNING

Lightning Source UK Ltd.
Milton Keynes UK
UKOW031817180912

199223UK00003B/8/P